BAD DECISIONS

INCLUDES DOG DAYS

SMALLTOWN SECRETS

CAT JOHNSON

Copyright © 2021 by Cat Johnson

BAD DECISIONS

1

CARSON

"Oh, deputy. Deputy Bekker!" The voice that managed to sound both frail and loud stopped me mid-step.

So close.

I'd made it halfway up the stairs and had almost gotten through the door of the Muddy River Inn. Had almost gotten a much-needed beer after a long day at work.

But it was not to be. Resigned to my fate, I turned.

Alice Mudd was half in and half out of Mary Brimley's car. The old lady clutched the passenger side doorframe of the vehicle with one hand and waved at me with the other.

Any other time, *during* my shift, I would have been happy to speak with the last member of Mudville's founding family who still lived in town.

As it was, my workday was over and, as sweet as

the ninety-plus year-old woman was, the last thing I wanted to do was go back down those steps and hear what she had to say.

Maybe I could put off whatever supposed urgent business Alice had to discuss with me until tomorrow.

Ha. Yeah. Good luck with that.

I knew my idea was wishful thinking. Even casual small talk with Mary and Alice could easily stretch out over an hour.

Meanwhile the aroma of frying food wafting out of the kitchen by way of the exhaust fan hit me. It was like a siren's song being piped into the parking lot to lure in passers-by.

Wistfully thinking about those hot wings I'd already started salivating over, I walked back down the few steps and forced a smile. "Yes, Alice?"

"We need to talk to you."

Obviously.

"All right. Do you want me to stop by your place tomorrow after my shift starts? Or would you rather come by the sheriff's department?" I offered.

She waved away my suggestions. "Oh goodness, no. This isn't sheriff's department business. This is personal."

I felt my brows creep up my forehead. "Oh?"

Personal? What in the world could this be about?

Not to be left out of the conversation, Mary Brimley stretched across the car from the driver's seat to peer past Alice so she could join in. "We wanted to know if you'd help us out with the centennial celebration for the library."

I drew in a breath. "How could I say no? Of course, I'll help."

Seriously. How could I have said no? They'd ambushed me and I didn't have a valid reason ready to get out of volunteering for the local event in the community that paid my salary with their tax dollars.

"Wonderful. We have a fabulous plan for a fundraiser that you'll be just perfect—"

"Mary!" Alice cut off her friend. "Let's surprise the deputy with the details later. At the planning meeting."

Ah, yes. With every event came the inevitable eternally long and all too frequent planning meetings.

My dread over having to attend this one was tempered when I saw a way out of this conversation. A clear path to the bar and that beer and wings. I'd just promise to talk to them about this at the meeting.

"Perfect. I'll be surprised at the meeting. See you ladies both there." I turned and covered the distance to the stairs in two long strides.

"Six o'clock tomorrow at the library," Alice hurried to add from behind me.

Without slowing down, I raised one arm in a wave and called back, "Got it. Thanks."

Pushing open the door and walking inside was like stepping into another world. The change from blinding hot summer sun to the cool, dim interior of the bar made me pause just inside the doorway for a moment.

The crack of balls colliding on the pool table was almost drowned out by the country song playing on the juke box as I headed toward the bar, still seeing spots as my eyes adjusted to the change in lighting.

I slid onto an empty barstool at the far end, hoping to limit further chitchat by putting myself in the corner, against the wall.

No one was behind the bar. I figured whoever was working today—either Carter or Laney—must be in the back grabbing a food order.

Hungry, I'd be sending whoever it was right back to the kitchen with my own order whenever they reappeared, which would hopefully be soon.

The door between the kitchen and the bar swung open and I was thrown into open-mouthed shock.

It wasn't Carter or Laney I saw, but she sure was a pleasant surprise.

She had dark hair—long, wavy and thick—that tumbled down her back. Tattooed on one arm from wrist to shoulder, she had more decorating her chest visible above the neckline of her tank top. The bold inked colors stood out in stark contrast against her milky, pale skin.

Wearing more rings than she had fingers as well as a small diamond nose stud that caught the light, it was clear she didn't shy away from adornment.

She wasn't from Mudville. That was for certain,

because I knew everyone in town and I'd know her if she were from here.

But she wasn't a complete stranger to me either. Last week I'd seen her walking into the bar when I'd been walking out. The entire encounter had lasted less than a minute, but I remembered it clearly. She'd made quite an impression.

Then, I'd figured she'd been just passing through. That, like quite a few of the bar's patrons, she'd hopped off the highway to grab a bite before getting on her way.

That she was standing behind the bar now proved I had guessed wrong.

I couldn't say I was upset about that. In a town of just over a thousand residents, with the majority of them eligible for their AARP card, this woman was a welcome addition.

Especially since the first time I'd seen her it had been after my last—and by last I meant final, as in no more—disastrous online date meet-up.

So, she'd been here looking for a job. That had to mean she was staying. Good to know.

Good in many ways.

As my gaze traveled from her black combat boots, over her fashionably ripped and faded jeans, and up over her sexy little white tank top, I finally hit on her face.

Dark brows arched high over blue—almost violet

—eyes only added to her annoyed expression as her mouth twisted.

"Did you need something?" she asked in a tone drenched in attitude.

Shit. I'd been caught checking her out. Me. The deputy in her new town. What kind of welcome was that?

A bad one.

At least I wasn't in uniform while behaving badly.

I'd gone right home after work. There, I found nothing good to eat or drink in the fridge. Rather than go shopping, I'd headed right here after I changed out of my uniform. Thank goodness for that.

"Uh, yeah. Thanks," I said in answer to her question about what I needed from her. "An order of hot wings. Extra spicy. Ranch instead of blue cheese. And a draft. Please. Thank you."

I'd added the last bit of extra politeness to hopefully redeem myself and my former bad behavior.

She nodded and turned toward the beer taps.

"You're new around here," I said to her back as she faced the taps.

"Mm-hm." She turned and planted the pint glass on a coaster in front of me without further comment, then pivoted toward the kitchen door.

I heard her calling my order out to whoever was cooking, then she was back, but no more talkative than before.

She grabbed a bar rag, picked up an empty beer

bottle at the other end of the bar, and wiped beneath it.

"Where did you move from?" I asked, determined to learn more.

"Not from around here." It seemed she was equally determined to keep me from my quest for information.

I was regrouping, trying to come up with my next line of questioning, when the tell-tale squeak and then slam of the front door behind me heralded a new arrival.

When I glanced over my shoulder to see who it was, she took the opportunity to disappear into the kitchen again.

"Carson. Good. You're here."

The elusive beauty would have to wait until later because Roger, the head of the library board, was making a beeline toward me from the door.

I'd have to reconsider my choice of locations for refreshment in my off-hours. I was doing more work here than I'd done at my desk during the final hour of my shift today.

I turned on the stool to fully face him. "Roger. What's up?"

"There's been a break-in at the library," he announced.

My eyes widened at that news. "Did you call the sheriff's department?"

"No."

"Why not?" I asked.

"Because you're here."

"So you came to the bar specifically looking for me to report it?" I asked.

"Well, no. I came here to pick up a takeout order. You just happened to be here."

I drew in a breath, realizing I definitely was going to have to start hiding after my shift or my workday would never end.

"Okay. Let's back up. When was the break in? Was anything taken?" I left the final question unspoken—that being why the hell didn't he just call the department?

He wobbled his head from side to side. "That's the thing. I'm not sure exactly what was taken. That would be impossible to tell without a full inventory of the collection."

I seriously doubted anyone would break into the public library to steal a book they could just borrow anyway.

"Is the computer, or petty cash or anything else that's not a book missing?" I asked, trying to reason out the possible motivation for this alleged robbery.

"No." Roger shook his head.

I probably should be grateful that crime in Mudville was so benign, but this sounded less and less like a break-in and more like paranoia.

"What evidence do you have someone broke in? Was the lock broken? Or a window?" I asked.

"No. *But*," he began with a dramatic flair, "the door was unlocked when I arrived this morning."

And yet he still didn't call it in this morning when I'd been at work…

Trying to get over that baffling detail, I resisted the impulse to reach for the notebook I always kept in my uniform pocket. I was no longer in uniform and that notebook was not in the pocket of my jeans because I was not supposed to be working now.

"Is it possible whoever closed last forgot to lock it?" I suggested.

"We've never forgotten to lock up before," he proclaimed with great pride and authority.

Plenty of things never happened, until they did… I left that thought also unspoken.

Meanwhile, the sexy stranger had returned.

I realized I still didn't know her name—and that would have been the perfect next question for her. I should have thought of it earlier.

More importantly, my wings were here and I was hungry.

They smelled so good I was literally drooling. All I wanted to do was eat them while they were still sizzling hot, but I still had Roger to deal with.

"I'll file a report in the morning," I offered, hoping to satisfy him before my food got cold and my beer warm.

"Please do. I want a record of this for when we do discover something's missing."

"Understood. I'll take care of it." *Tomorrow.*

"Kayleigh! Order up!" Carter yelled from the kitchen, causing the girl to spin toward the door again.

Kayleigh...

"Is that my order?" Roger called after her.

She ignored him as she disappeared through the doorway and into the kitchen.

Apparently, I'd been dismissed by Roger in favor of his takeout order. And not a moment too soon because the stranger now had a name and I intended to take advantage of it.

2

KAYLEIGH

People in this town never shut up.

Until I'd suffered the townies in Mudville I'd thought my relatives talked a lot. But these people might have my big Irish family beat.

Sunday dinner back at home in Charlestown could be a chaotic experience with my two brothers, mother, father, Grandma Walsh, and sometimes even Father O'Malley from St. Mary's, all talking at once.

Things got especially loud when my Uncle James or my cousins would come to join us. Then Sunday dinner turned into a real free for all.

Thoughts of my family brought back the heavy feeling in my chest.

Ma was probably losing her mind about my being gone. Grandma would be stoically silent and Dad would be quietly simmering mad. And through it all, I could picture my brother Connor playing peacemaker. Defending me and my sudden departure.

Memories of those loud, mandatory Sunday family dinners were making me homesick.

As brave as I pretended to be, I still couldn't deny I missed everyone and everything so much. It was my first time being this far away from home. Even college hadn't been so far.

But even if I were home right this very second, Declan wouldn't be there. I pushed that painful thought aside.

He was the reason I was here. And the reason I needed to focus on my task.

Keeping my goal in mind, I tried to tune in to a conversation happening at a nearby table to see if I could pick up any new information.

It had been surprisingly easy to learn about everything in this town just in my short time behind the bar. Like I said, people here talked. And talked. I listened and learned, so I didn't mind all the chatter... except for all the personal questions directed at me.

I wasn't in this bumfuck town to make friends or get to know people.

Growing up, I'd been taught from a young age to keep things close to the vest. Avoid questions when possible and keep answers vague.

That was true now, more than ever. Especially when the hot guy with the dirty-blond hair seated at the bar asked those questions.

Unlike the old ladies' gossipy queries, his questions felt different.

My best guess was that he was some sort of off-duty law enforcement.

That assumption was based on the conversation he had with the rude old guy who didn't even thank me for getting his takeout order.

But there was one critical piece of information I'd gleaned from the hottie with the body whose kaleidoscope eyes I kept finding focused on me. It was the tidbit that Mr. Takeout-Order had dropped to Hot Cop.

The information that had my heart pounding… Somebody had been in the library last night—or maybe the old guy had just forgotten to lock up.

If it was the former, it could be the lead, the verification, that I needed that Declan was here. If it were the latter, I was still at zero in my search here in Mudville.

Of all the places in the world my search could have led me, this town was the last place I would have guessed I'd end up.

Turning, I saw the hot guy's eyes were on me again as he wiped the extra spicy hot wing sauce from his fingers with the wet nap.

I batted away the errant thought that he too looked extra hot and spicy.

Not the time. Not the place. And if he was a cop,

definitely *not* the man for me to be indulging in to satisfy my baser needs.

Screwing a cop would be too dangerous. That didn't mean he wasn't as tempting as he was off-limits.

"Yoo-hoo! Deputy Bekker." The old lady's summons, called from across the room directly to my fantasy man, confirmed my theory.

Deputy Bekker.

Yup. He was a lawman and I had very good reason to be avoiding him.

Saddened by that, I watched as he drew in a breath, as if bracing himself for the encounter before he turned on the bar stool to face her.

"Yes, Mrs. Trout?"

His smile looked forced.

My smile wasn't. The old lady bothering him kind of brightened my mood since the deputy had been bothering me in one way or another since walking in here.

By sitting at my bar looking so damn good.

By asking too many damn questions.

By making me want to jump him…

He was a distraction I didn't need or want right now but at least his day hadn't been all roses either between rude takeout guy and this insistent old bag.

"We wanted to ask you—" the old lady began.

"If I'd help out with the centennial celebration committee. Alice and Mary already told me all about it." He nodded.

"Oh, good. You'll be perfect."

"That's exactly what they said. I'm going to get a swelled head from all these compliments," he joked, while all I could focus on was the image of another body part on this man swelling.

Apparently, I'd developed a one-track mind centering around sex. Or at least sex with this man.

Is this what extreme stress and worry did to a woman's libido? Ramped it up into the danger zone?

"So there's a lot to do and only weeks to do it all before the event. We have lists and lists. That's why we're starting the bi-weekly meetings tomorrow night."

"Bi-weekly? Meaning every two weeks?" he asked, hopeful.

"Oh, goodness no. Too much to do for that. Twice a week."

There was a flash of disappointment in his eyes before he said, "Oh. Great."

I smothered my burst of a laugh at his thinly veiled sarcasm.

Meanwhile, his gaze cut to the door. "Looks like Mr. Trout is waiting for you."

Mrs. Trout waved off his observation. "With as long as we've been married, he should know better than to try and rush a woman. But you'll learn that when you finally find a nice girl and settle down."

"No doubt." He nodded with another forced smile.

So, Deputy Bekker hadn't already found a nice girl to settle down with. Interesting.

I was a nice girl. Kind of. Okay, at least I was trying.

"Meeting is at six. Do. Not. Be. Late. We have lots to discuss and I don't want to be there past nine when my program comes on the television." She'd actually poked him as she spoke the warning.

Silly me was envious of that finger getting to touch his well-muscled chest.

"I'll be on time," he said with more patience than I could have shown in the face of that meeting.

Three hours, in a room filled with people just like annoying Mrs. Trout? This man was a saint if he could deal with that.

I was starting to feel sorry for the guy who—besides interrogating me—seemed only interested in eating his meal and enjoying his beer in peace.

Poor man hadn't gotten to do either with all the interruptions.

"Margaret!"

"Oh, good God. Hold your horses. I'm coming." She scowled at her husband, who was holding the door open, as if that would make her move faster.

His wife wasn't moving, but one big horse fly took advantage of Mr. Trout's hospitality.

I watched it zoom inside, cross the room and dive bomb into the mirror behind me. It fell, stunned, behind all the liquor bottles on the shelves against the mirror.

Great.

"See you tomorrow. Remember. Six, sharp." She'd repeated that warning before turning toward the door.

Carson let out a breath as he watched her leave. Then slowly, as if he'd lost all will to live, he turned back toward the bar and reached for his beer.

His hand froze when he saw I'd topped off his glass while he'd been talking to the Trout woman.

"You looked like you needed a refill after that," I explained, tipping my chin in the direction of the exit where the Trouts were now arguing just outside the door.

He sniffed out a laugh.

"You're not wrong." After a long swallow of beer, he said, "Thank you."

"My pleasure." And it was, which was bad. Very bad.

He smiled and damned if I didn't feel my pulse speed at the sight.

Crud.

I should be steering clear of the law. Clear of him.

Or maybe not. What was that saying? Keep your friends close and your enemies closer.

Maybe it wouldn't be a bad thing to keep the hot deputy close.

That I really liked the idea of being close to him should have been a warning sign that I should run the other way. Instead, I was too busy thinking his lips were really pretty.

"I'm Carson Bekker," he said with a smile.

I knew that already. Between Mr. Rude Takeout, who had called him by his first name, and the old lady, who had called him by his last name, I had already pieced it all together.

My paranoia had me second-guessing—and third-guessing—Carson's motives.

Was he flirting? Or hoping I'd supply my full name in return so he could investigate me?

Or maybe he was just being polite, like I'd seen him do with every person who'd bothered him so far.

The reality was he could just ask the owner of the bar who I was if he really wanted to dig deeper.

If he dug, he'd only find what I wanted him to. The name I'd applied for the job under was only partially mine. Good luck tracing me from that.

After a longer pause than the question warranted, I answered, "I'm Kayleigh."

First name only. That was all he was going to get from me. Let him work for the rest if he wanted to know so badly.

He smiled. "I know. I heard Carter calling you before. I'm happy to meet you, Kayleigh."

Pfft. Of course he had heard my name with Carter bellowing it from the kitchen every time there was an order ready.

I'd forgotten that little detail, proving I really was

off my game. The deputy had thrown me off. That fact was even more dangerous to my well-being than the handsome deputy.

"Uh. Yeah. Happy to meet you too," I lied, barely managing to keep up my part in this simple conversation.

Happy to see the law. Yeah. Not in this lifetime.

Cozying up to Carson the lawman was a very bad idea…and I was going to do it anyway.

3

CARSON

My evening wasn't turning out too badly after all.

Yes, thanks to not one but two encounters with the old biddies—as Red and her friends liked to call the more senior ladies of Mudville—I'd be attending a meeting I didn't want to go to tomorrow night.

But I also now had a name to go with the enticing female behind the bar.

Kayleigh… I liked it.

Hell, I liked her. And I hadn't felt that way about a woman in at least a year.

Definitely not during any of my online dates.

Not since I'd asked Red out—finally—after dancing around her in the friend zone since we'd been in the same graduating class in high school.

But since she was already half in love with Cashel

Morgan at the time that I'd asked her out, in the friend zone I'd remain forevermore.

But Kayleigh—she didn't have a history in this town.

She hadn't grown up with me. Hadn't graduated from Mudville High. Hadn't already dated a bunch of guys I'd known forever.

Most importantly, she hadn't known me during those awkward, pimply, teen years when I'd sprouted up over six feet while weighing about a buck-fifty soaking wet.

She was one of a very limited number of young, attractive single females in a small town that was aging rapidly upwards. And I for one was very happy to have her as a new addition to the Mudville population.

Carter pushed through the kitchen doorway and stepped behind the bar. He shot Kayleigh a wide smile, showing his full set of white teeth. Like a shark circling its prey.

I didn't want to think the words *fresh meat*, but they flew into my brain anyway.

Shit. I had to move fast or I'd lose her to Carter.

Single, handsome, just a couple of years younger than me and Laney's son, so also heir apparent to the Muddy River Inn, he was a definite contender. A worthy opponent for Kayleigh's attentions. And dammit I wanted all her attention on me.

My best bet seemed to be to distract Carter.

We were kind of friends. I'd known him since he'd been a kid, and I'd been a slightly older kid.

I'd come here to eat sometimes with my grandmother. Carter had always been here after school and on weekends while Laney, a single mother, worked with her son underfoot until the night shift employee came on.

"Hey, Carter," I called.

He lifted a chin to me and, after sidling past Kayleigh, finally made his way to my end of the bar. "Hey, Carson. What's going on with you?"

"Same old, same old. The ladies in town roped me into helping out with the planning for the centennial celebration for the library."

Carter laughed out loud. "Dude. You gotta learn to avoid those women."

"They cornered me in the parking lot." I shook my head. "I didn't have a choice."

"That's why I park behind the building and slip in the kitchen door."

Damn. I should have thought of that myself. "Good idea. I might have to start doing that too."

Carter's dark brow cocked up. "Nope. Don't do it. Laney doesn't like customers in her kitchen."

I'd long gotten used to Carter calling his mother by her first name at the bar. That didn't mean I liked what he was saying to me.

"Okay. Fine. I'll just have to take my chances in the parking lot." My gaze hit on the female behind Carter and I decided to see what I could find out. "So, uh... new employee?"

His grin spread wide. "You noticed that did you?"

"Hard to miss," I admitted.

"You ain't kidding. Yup. She came in looking for a job last week."

The timing fit. That would have been the day that I'd seen her coming in when I'd been walking out.

"What do you know about her?" I realized my question came out sounding more like a deputy was asking, and in a way, it was as much professional interest as personal that had me making the inquiry.

Yeah, I wouldn't mind taking her out and getting to know her a whole lot better. Which would hopefully lead to much more. But I also was more than curious about what would make an attractive young woman choose Mudville as the place to tend bar.

She'd make ten times as many tips working in one of the towns with big state universities nearby. Oneonta. Binghamton. Syracuse. Albany.

Or, if college bars weren't her thing, she could still find a better place to work than here.

I loved this place, but it was without a doubt a towny dive bar, filled with locals, many on fixed incomes.

If she worked instead at a fancy place filled with tourists, like maybe the Otesaga or someplace near Cooperstown, she'd clean up. There, the dinner and drink bill totals were sky high, so the tips would be high as well.

If my question did sound suspicious to him, Carter didn't let on. His lips twitched as he said, "Interested in her, are ya?"

I lifted one shoulder and smiled in acknowledgment of the truth. "Do you blame me?"

"Not at all. But there's not much I can tell you. My mother interviewed her for the job. There's bare minimum on her application."

"You checked?" I asked.

Carter raised one shoulder. "Hey. Can't blame a guy for doing a little research."

Since I was doing the same, no, I couldn't blame Carter for checking out her application.

"Where's she living? Do you know?"

There were rentals around here, but not a whole lot.

The village proper itself was small. Small in both population and square miles. Of course, she could be living in one of the neighboring towns.

"Upstairs, actually," Carter supplied.

I lifted a brow. "She's living upstairs here?"

"Yup. My mother finally got the attic apartment cleared of junk. A coat of paint and some furniture from the consignment shop and it doesn't look too bad up there." He leaned closer. "Looks a whole lot better with her in it. I can tell you that."

I nodded in agreement, as well as in a show of male solidarity, while processing that information.

Meanwhile, Kayleigh was watching me. Or maybe both of us—Carter and me. Probably because it was obvious we were talking about her.

My grandmother must be rolling in her grave. She had raised me better than to talk about a woman behind her back. Or right in front of her, as the case may be.

But damn, I was curious. And, yes, interested in her. On so many levels.

The bar's phone rang and I had the opportunity to watch Kayleigh unobserved as she answered. I glanced up and saw Carter doing the same.

When he realized I'd caught him staring, he grinned.

"You going to ask her out?" I asked, deciding it would only help me to know what I was up against.

"Nah." Carter shook his head. "Laney already made it clear. Threatened me, actually. Hands off the employees. Usually, that's not a problem since between my mother and my cousin who helps out, I'm related to most of them. But this time..." Carter let the sentence trail off while he shot a wistful glance at Kayleigh.

This was very good news. Not for Carter, of course. But for me? Yeah. I couldn't have asked for better. His loss was my gain.

"You?" Carter asked.

"Me what?" I turned my attention back to him.

"Are you going to ask her out?" Carter clarified.

Not liking the turn this conversation had taken as he put me on the spot, I shrugged. "I haven't decided yet."

"Why the hell not? What's there to decide?" His voice rose as high as his brows.

I dared to cast a glance in her direction, hoping she hadn't heard any of this conversation.

It looked like I was in luck. The music was loud and she was still talking to a customer on the phone.

Good. While she was busy at the other end of the bar, bent over scribbling something on a paper, she wasn't listening to us.

"I'm not sure she's interested, is all." As much as I didn't like this conversation, I still chose the truth.

Kayleigh didn't have the warm and fuzzies when it came to me. Or anyone, for that matter. I could feel the wall built solid and high around her.

I'd seen the wary look she'd given me when I'd first arrived.

But then she had warmed up a bit, giving me that second beer, so maybe I was off base.

Who knew? Women were confusing as fuck.

"Dude. I'm not allowed to take her out, but if I were, you can bet your badge I would already be on it," Carter continued, still obsessed over my lack of commitment when it came to asking out the woman

I'd only officially met all of an hour ago. "You have nothing stopping you. I *insist* you make a move."

"You insist, do you?" I laughed at his fervor. "Since you're so invested, where do you suggest I ask her out to?"

My go-to place for all my ill-fated online dating meetups had been here.

Given that Kayleigh worked here, that was out.

Prying eyes and local town gossip aside, I didn't think she'd want to come out from behind the bar just to sit in front of it with me. That didn't seem like much of a night out for her.

Carter rolled his eyes. "Come on. Do I gotta do everything for you? You could go to Mudville House. The diner. The drive-in movies. Honey Buns. It all depends what you're looking to do on a first date."

He'd ticked off the many choices on his fingers, proving I did have options.

"Now, if you want hot and heavy with a big investment, I'd go for Mudville House. Cheap and quick? Then it's the diner. Daytime date, I'd hit Honey Buns. You want a few hours alone in the dark, I'd choose the drive-in. In fact, that would definitely be my choice." He waggled his eyebrows suggestively.

Damn him. Now I'd started to think about what could happen there in the dark in my car with Kayleigh during a late-night double feature. It was a tempting image.

He leveled a stare on me. "And, you know, you are allowed to actually cross the town line."

I rolled my eyes. "I know that."

"There are a bunch of places to go if you don't mind driving twenty-minutes. Hell, the Otesaga is just an hour away. That place is a panty dropper if ever I saw one."

Great. Now I was picturing Kayleigh's panties.

He shook his head and continued, "You're just being dumb. And stubborn. Why, I don't know. It'd be a no brainer for me."

"All right. I hear you. I'll... consider it."

Carter opened his mouth, no doubt to call me out on my continued hesitation, when Kayleigh hung up the phone and said, "Carter, I've got a takeout order."

"All right." He groaned and glanced back at me. "Duty calls. I'm cooking until Laney gets in. Then I get to take over behind the bar until closing."

As far as jobs went, it didn't seem all that horrible to have to hang out at a bar all night and get paid to do it. Though I knew it had its challenges.

I decided to throw Carter a bone since he didn't look all that thrilled to be working today.

"Well, the hot wings you made me were excellent," I said.

He snorted. "Thanks."

On his way to the kitchen, he paused to grab the slip with the order on it as he said to Kayleigh, "As soon as my mom gets in, you can head out."

She nodded as he shoved open the door to the kitchen. That left Kayleigh here. Alone. With me.

It was my golden opportunity. "Um, I should settle up before your shift ends. You wanna cash me out?"

"Yeah. Sure." She delivered another small white piece of paper to me.

I glanced at the total then tossed a twenty on the bar.

As she scooped up the cash, I said, "So, any fun plans for the evening when you get out of here?"

It was an obvious and far from smooth ploy, but I couldn't come up with anything better.

Maybe I was the one who fell short on all my recent bad dates and not the women from the matchmaking sites.

I'd have to think on that more later. Right now, I was waiting for Kayleigh to return from the cash register. More than that, I was waiting for her answer.

She returned with my change. I waved it off. "Keep it."

"Thanks." She stuffed it into the tip jar behind her and then turned back to me. "No plans. I was just going to go upstairs and hang in my apartment. You, uh, wanna come up?"

I felt my eyes pop wide.

Had she really just asked me back to her place? The apartment directly overhead. Right up the exterior stairs. The steps that were in plain sight of anyone in the parking lot?

I had to get over that fact and moved on to the other shocking revelation in her invitation. She didn't dislike me after all, in spite of those looks she'd shot me at the start of the evening.

My mouth was hanging open. When I realized that, I consciously closed it.

Meanwhile, I still had yet to answer her.

It shouldn't be a hard question to answer. God knew what I wanted to do. Still, there seemed to be a lot of shit going on in my head.

Maybe she was just being social. She must be lonely, being a new girl in a strange town.

Yeah, this was just a visit. Of course, it was. She hadn't said to come up for sex or anything crazy like that.

How silly of me.

Getting over the shock and finally thinking rationally, I nodded. "Uh, yeah. Sure. I'll come up. I'd love to."

4

KAYLEIGH

Friends close. Enemies closer.

Although Carson Bekker was not my enemy, as a man of the law he could do harm to someone I loved. Someone I was willing to do anything for. Including *that*...

It wouldn't be so bad, if it came to that. To say Carson was an attractive guy would be a huge understatement.

He was the kind of guy who I would have walked up to at a party or a bar. I would have flirted my ass off with a man like Carson—at any other time.

Hell, I might have even taken him home.

How was this any different?

He was hot. He was nice. He was employed—not that I was looking for a good provider to marry or anything. Just saying, the guys that I knew from home who had legitimate, income tax-paying jobs were few and far between.

And Carson held the keys to unlock possible information that could help.

So what if I did end up sleeping with him?

Women liked sex too. And I was a woman who hadn't gotten any in what felt like forever.

That's what happened when your world imploded. Things like having any sort of a personal life fell by the wayside.

I'd had two boyfriends in college. And I could honestly say both put the emphasis on the word *boy* in boyfriend when it came to sex.

Tonight, for the right reasons or the wrong ones, my dry spell could come to an end. And with the hot deputy, who definitely was a man and who I hoped would come with the added benefit of providing some much-needed information at the same time.

Two birds. One stone. Climaxes and crime reports. I liked it. The perfect combination for my upside-down life.

After a long day behind the bar, I was ready to get out of here. But poor Deputy Carson looked like he was about to swallow his tongue when I'd suggested he come upstairs.

He had the essence of a choir boy about him, in spite of his being hot as hell and all man, right down to his bulging forearms and well-defined chest.

It was a dichotomy I found oddly fascinating. And irresistibly attractive.

Another time, another situation, and he and I might have a chance at something. As it was, I was about to use this man for my own purposes. And I was desperate enough to not feel bad about it.

While I waited for Carter to come out to take over the bar and shoved my tips into my bag I found myself tingling with nerves and anticipation. And tingling in places that hadn't tingled in a while.

I hid a smile as I saw Carson nursing the last sip of his beer while he waited for me to be able to leave. He looked pretty nervous himself.

Finally, the kitchen door swung open and Carter came through the doorway. "Okay. I got the bar. You're good to go."

"Thank you." I smiled.

For the first time since moving in just a few days ago I was not dreading going upstairs alone to my one room in the attic with the weak, though free, WiFi.

I grabbed my bag and walked around the bar, pausing by Carson. "Ready?"

His gaze cut to Carter before he focused on me. "Yeah."

I didn't miss the lift of my new coworker's eyebrows as he watched the deputy and I walk out the front door together.

Carter couldn't see us turn the corner and ascend

the exterior stairs to my apartment, but he'd see both my car and Carson's vehicle still in the lot.

He was a smart guy. He'd figure it out and make his own assumptions. Ask me if I cared. I didn't.

Carter hadn't asked me out so he shouldn't care either way. Not that I would have said yes to him.

I truly didn't need or want emotional entanglements in Mudville. That wasn't why I was here. Lucky for me, getting close to Carson fit the need of why I was here.

It was summer, so the sun was up and glaring, even if it was evening. It felt a bit naughty to be bringing home a man to my apartment in broad daylight. But I wasn't going to let that stop me.

I closed the door on the sun and decided to ignore it.

He glanced around as I closed us inside.

The space felt even smaller with him in it. Making it almost hard to breathe. I didn't mind. Although the narrow bed was going to be extra crowded with him in it with me.

That thought had my heart pounding.

Okay, maybe I was as nervous as Carson looked.

"So, uh, nice room. I've never been up—" Carson didn't finish his banal comment about the attic bedroom I was renting for a bargain price above the bar.

I had taken a step forward until we were only a breath apart.

His gaze dropped to watch as I ran my hands over his chest before he brought his eyes up to focus on mine.

I took another step, which had us touching each other. I heard as well as saw him swallow hard. His nervousness made me smile. It also made me bolder.

Leaning in, I closed the short distance. I wasn't fast enough.

He pulled back, breaking any chance of contact between us.

"You wanna grab something to eat?" he asked.

"You just ate," I pointed out, surprised at his avoidance.

"Yeah. But that was just an appetizer." He treated me to an adorable, crooked smile.

"It was a *dozen* wings," I emphasized the word dozen to prove my point.

"I thought you might be hungry after working all day," he continued.

"Oh, I am hungry." I moved closer again and ran my hands down his chest, trying my best to be an irresistible siren. One no man could turn down.

I was completely out of my wheelhouse here.

Meanwhile, with my hands on his chest like this, I couldn't help thinking how this man definitely worked out. He was rocking pecs of steel, hard beneath my palms until he grabbed my hands.

He held them, halting my journey down toward his waistband.

"I want to take you out. On a proper date," he said.

I felt my brows rise. Had I found myself a proper gentleman?

In this day and age, I hadn't thought that was possible. But if it were possible anywhere, it would be here in Mudville.

From what I'd seen of the town in my short time here, with its big old stately houses from the turn of the century and its citizens that might be just as old, if a gentleman existed, he'd live here.

I knew the old folks couldn't have actually lived through the Victorian era, but there were a few at least who looked like it.

This man, who couldn't be over thirty, might as well have been a Victorian gentleman trying not to sully my honor.

Little did he know, the only honor where I came from meant not being a rat to save your own skin when the police questioned you.

Carson was who he was. And if I wanted to get close to him, I had to accept that and work with it. He wanted a date. I could do a date.

"Sure. I could eat," I said.

My answer brought a smile to his face. "Good. Where do you want to go?"

I didn't even need to think before I said, "Not downstairs."

He smiled wider. "Yeah. I figured that. What are you in the mood for?"

If I told him I was in the mood for sex, what would this boy scout of a man do? Probably run back down the stairs.

"We have Chinese and pizza in the next town over," he continued, listing the few culinary offerings of the area. "But as for here in town, it's pretty slim pickings. There's Mudville House, but they're not open today. There's the diner right on Main Street. They're open early for breakfast and late for dinner—"

"Will you still be here in the morning to have breakfast?" I asked.

He stared at me as if waiting to see if I was serious or not. I smiled and pretended I'd been joking.

Looking relieved, he smiled back and then said, "So what will it be?"

"Pizza, Chinese or the diner?" I asked, reviewing my choices.

He nodded.

"How many of the people I served today are gonna be there at the diner?" I asked.

He sniffed. "Probably all of them. Like I said, it's pretty much the only game in town midweek. Besides here."

The last thing I wanted to do was see the locals I'd spent the day trying to please. "Then Chinese it is."

"Good choice. Ready to go?" he asked.

"Sure."

He opened the door for me, then stepped back and waited for me to walk through. I had no doubt he'd open the car door for me as well. I had indeed found myself a gentleman.

A deputy and a gentleman. I only hoped I didn't regret one or both of those things when this whole thing was over.

And jeez, I hoped it would be over soon.

CARSON

An actual date. It wasn't what I'd been anticipating when I'd walked into the Muddy River Inn after my shift to get a beer and some wings.

Then again, I'd never imagined seeing the new mystery woman in town behind that bar either. Nor could I ever in a million years have guessed Kayleigh would invite me upstairs to her apartment.

The only thing more shocking, I suppose, was the fact that I didn't take advantage of that.

Nope. Instead, I'd dragged her back out. And to a public place for a meal that I didn't need or want, rather than stay in that room with her.

A room. Her. And a bed. The combination of those things had sent me running for the door, when most men would have been salivating just at the idea of it.

What the hell was wrong with me?

I liked women. I liked sex. A lot, actually. Yet I couldn't get out of her room fast enough.

Sometimes I wish I could just flick that angel off my one shoulder and listen to the devil on the other one. The devil whispering in my ear to just go for it. To take what she was so obviously offering and enjoy it.

Instead, I'd fled the attic room. Ran away from the quaint space with the low, pitched ceiling and faded handmade quilt on the bed. Had gotten as far away from the narrow bed with the antique brass headboard as I could.

I'd fled all the way across the county line to the next town, choosing Chow Fun Lo Mein rather than fun in bed with Kayleigh.

"Do you want to come upstairs?" Kayleigh asked me for the second time tonight.

This time, she held the brown paper bag of Chinese leftovers in one hand as we stood next to my SUV, parked at the bar.

Instead of saying yes. That I'd love to go upstairs with her. Instead of sprinting up the staircase, busting through the door and getting both of us naked before we hit the bed, I said, "I'll walk you up and see you safely inside before I head home."

Her dark brows rose and an amused smile twitched her lips. "You really are a boy scout, aren't you?"

A bark of a laugh escaped me at her accurate assessment. "I guess so. Sorry."

I hadn't planned on still acting like a boy scout at thirty but apparently, I was.

Freaking Boy Scouts.

She probably didn't realize, but I sure did, that it was very possibly my decade plus in that organization that had done this to me. Made me forever a scout at heart.

It made me feel better to blame my inconvenient sense of honor on Mudville's Troop One. On my achieving Eagle Scout before I aged out of the organization.

That idea was easier to swallow than admitting my failures as a man in the romance department.

Her gaze met and held mine for a beat before her mouth tipped up in a smile.

Shaking her head, she said, "Don't apologize. I'm starting to like it."

That admission brought on a grin I couldn't seem to control. "Yeah?"

"Yeah," she echoed on a sigh, making her sound resigned and a shade unhappy about it. "Come on. Walk me up."

She tipped her head toward the stairs while reaching for the railing and starting the ascent.

I followed her up. I guess I wasn't completely a boy scout after all since I did watch her hips sway in those sexy jeans of hers.

At the top, she unlocked the door and swung it wide, peeking inside herself before turning back to me.

"All clear, deputy." She even went so far as to execute a messy salute with her report.

"Good to hear. Though you didn't look in the bathroom or under the bed."

She pulled her mouth to one side. "I'm not all that worried. Seriously. What kind of crime can there be around here in Mudville?"

"You'd be surprised." I'd pretty much seen it all in my years with the department. Break-ins and trespassing. Robberies. Mysteriously missing livestock…

"You mean crime sprees such as the old guy who thinks the library was broken into because the door wasn't locked?" she asked.

I laughed at her assessment of Roger. "Yup."

"Do you think it was? An intruder, I mean. Or did he just forget to lock up?" she asked, sounding genuinely interested.

I couldn't blame her if she were concerned. She was a woman living alone in a new town in an apartment that had no neighbors or anyone nearby each night after the bar closed.

"I don't know." I shook my head. "I'll have to look into it tomorrow."

"What do you think it was though? You must have

a guess," she prompted. Again, sounding more interested than I thought the topic warranted.

It was the library. The only thing of real value inside was the computer and Roger hadn't said that was missing or anything noticeably disturbed.

I wasn't even sure how to go about investigating it.

Maybe the neighbor's security camera caught something, because it wasn't like I could dust for prints. It was a public space. We held meetings there, once a week or more. Half the town was in and out of that door on any given week.

Still, Kayleigh had asked me a question and I had to try to give her an answer, even if I didn't really have one.

"Honestly, right now, going only on what I know—which isn't much—it's fifty-fifty in my mind. Someone could have been in there. It wouldn't be the first time we've had squatters. Though they usually leave some evidence behind and Roger didn't mention any. So it could be just as likely someone forgot to lock up when they left last night." I shrugged.

Kayleigh nodded while looking distracted.

At the sight of her frown, I asked, "Are you worried? I was joking before but I'm more than happy to come in and check the bathroom and under the bed. And make sure your locks are strong and secure—"

"I'm not worried. I'll be fine. Thanks." She took a step inside and turned back to me. She lifted the bag.

"Thank you for dinner and for the leftovers. Maybe I'll see you tomorrow."

Holy whiplash, Batman.

She'd gone from practically dragging me inside before dinner, to inviting me upstairs after dinner, to now—standing with her hand on the door and looking as if she were waiting for me to leave so she could slam it.

"Oh. Okay. Yeah. You have my number in your phone in case you need anything," I reminded her.

She tipped her head. "I do. Thanks."

Kayleigh indulged me with the smallest of smiles. It seemed forced. Polite. Nothing more.

Shit. I'd missed my shot.

I'd dragged my feet and now, for some reason, she was over it. Over me.

Even though she'd said she found my boy scout ways endearing, she must have just been humoring me. Because the woman in front of me now couldn't wait for me to get the hell off her doorstep.

I could feel the waning patience radiating off her, increasing with every passing second.

"All right. Well, good night," I said.

"Good night, Carson." She pushed the door closed before I'd even turned to head down the stairs.

My feet felt heavy as I made my way down, my mind spinning with what had happened. Where exactly I'd gone wrong.

"Well, well, well." Carter's voice brought my head up.

I stifled a grown when I saw him standing there, a large black trash bag in one hand.

He stood at the bottom of the stairs grinning up at me as I descended the final two steps to reach ground level.

That I happened to be skulking away from Kayleigh's apartment at the exact moment Carter left his post behind the bar to take out the garbage was proof, a physical manifestation, of exactly how unlucky I was.

"I see somebody got smart and finally decided to man up and sample the new dish in town," he continued, still grinning as he moved to the corner of the building and tossed the bag into the dumpster.

Following him, I sniffed. Oh, how wrong he was. I wasn't smart. Far from it.

A smart man would have tumbled into Kayleigh's bed when she invited him and stayed until one or both of us needed to go to work.

Instead, I'd be driving home alone tonight with nothing for company but the strong suspicion that after her chilly goodbye there wouldn't be another invitation.

I'd missed my chance.

"You have the wrong idea," I said, correcting him.

"Sure." Carter's single word was ripe with sarcasm.

The more I denied it, the more he'd think I was

lying. But it wasn't in me to leave while he still had the wrong impression.

I tried again to convince him of the truth. "I took her to get Chinese food in Sidney then walked her upstairs and said good night. Nothing more."

Carter let out a snort and I feared he still didn't believe me, until he shook his head and said, "You're such a frigging boy scout."

That seemed to be the general consensus.

"Yup." I agreed then lifted my hand in a half-hearted wave. "Goodnight, Carter."

This boy scout was going home. Alone. Maybe I could dig out my old badges in the attic. They could keep me company tonight.

6

KAYLEIGH

I shoved the bag of leftovers in the tiny dorm room sized fridge that came with my apartment, then raced back to the door. I held my breath and listened to the sound of Carson's footsteps as he descended the stairs.

After he reached the bottom and I didn't hear his boots on the wooden steps anymore, I counted to ten to give him time to walk to his car and drive away.

Only then did I grab my keys and dare to crack open the door.

Sticking my head out, I peered down the staircase. The coast seemed to be clear. I pulled the door closed, making sure it was locked and then trotted down the rickety wooden steps as fast as I dared.

I was about to round the corner and head for my car when I heard it. The murmur of two male voices. I pressed close to the building to avoid being seen and dared to peek around the corner.

Carter and Carson stood talking next to the stinky dumpster, of all places.

Shit. I pulled back and leaned against the wall, out of sight.

I needed them to leave so I could go too. I had to get to the library before full dark and find someplace to hide where I could see the door and wait.

Wait, watch and hope.

Hope that there really was an intruder and not a forgetful library employee. Hope that whoever had broken in would be back again tonight.

And, most importantly, hope that it was who I suspected.

But I couldn't go anywhere with these two guys blocking the path to my car. There would be too much explaining to do.

Ugh!

Carter was supposed to be behind the bar and Carson, I assumed, had a home to get back to. So why were they still standing there?

Finally, I heard Carson say goodnight. Then I heard the slam of the kitchen door as Carter went back inside.

I waited for the sound of an engine and the crunch of tires on the gravel before I peeked around the corner again. Carson's white SUV was turning onto the main road.

A few seconds later, he was out of sight. I took that opportunity to trot to my car and slip inside.

Town was close, but too far to walk. Driving, even at the thirty mile an hour limit, I covered the two miles in no time.

Slowing, I passed the library. I pulled along the curb a bit farther down the block so my car wouldn't be suspiciously parked directly in front of the building during the hours it was closed.

I cut the engine and lights and slid down in the seat. I could see the front door. The question was, was there also a back door?

The old guy had said the door was unlocked but I don't think he specified which door.

It was obvious that I wasn't well versed in investigations. I hadn't majored in criminal justice at UMass.

In hindsight, and given my family's sordid history, that was probably a mistake. The thought had been to get as far away from the criminal underworld as I could. But that world seemed determined to keep dragging me, and my family, back into it.

Sighing, I realized I should have brought something to drink with me. Coffee. Water. Soda. And something to pee inside, too, if it came to that. This could be a very long night.

Or maybe not.

The light caught my attention first, before the dark

shadow of a man appeared attached to that flashlight beam.

I gripped the steering wheel and pulled myself forward, closer to the windshield I so anxiously peered through.

Could it be him? Declan.

My heart thundered at the thought as I watched the figure move to the door and reach for the knob. Then the person made their way slowly around the building, looking as if they were checking the ground level windows.

Finally, he strode down the sidewalk toward the parking lot—and toward a big white boxy vehicle I recognized. I should. I'd just been inside it.

I let out the breath I hadn't realized I'd been holding.

Not Declan. But instead, Carson.

Of course, it was him. His actions fit perfectly with what I'd learned from knowing him for just one day.

Even off-duty, he wouldn't be able to go home and rest for the night without checking on the library. Making sure it was secure.

I slumped down low in the seat again as he pulled the SUV out of the parking lot and took a disturbingly long time to finally drive away.

It wasn't until he was out of sight that I relaxed again. I didn't have a good excuse for being here. And I knew from experience he was a question-asker.

My heart had just finally slowed to normal when

the ringing of my cell phone had me jumping out of my skin. I wrestled it out of my pocket and read the name on the screen.

Connor.

I'd been dodging calls from my brother and my mother for days. In fact, I hadn't talked to anyone from home since making the decision to leave and look for Declan.

They couldn't know where I was or I had no doubt someone would have been sent to drag me back home days ago. But I also knew they'd be worried. And if I kept not answering, they could assume the worst.

What if they blamed the wrong people for my disappearance? That could spiral into a war that could cost me more than I'd already lost.

Making a split-second decision, I swiped to answer the call before it went to voicemail.

"Connor." My voice sounded breathless in my own ears.

My brother let out a long string of obscenities that would have earned him fifty Hail, Marys at confession before he said, "Kayleigh, where are you?"

The controlled calm in his question told me he was holding on to his temper by a thread.

"I can't tell you." And he wouldn't be able to find out either. I'd been careful. Taken precautions.

I'd turned off all location services and installed a VPN on my cell phone to make sure they couldn't easily track me.

Sure, if they got the cops involved, they could subpoena the phone records and find which cell towers my phone had pinged on. But if I knew one thing about my family, they didn't go to the cops. The cops usually came to us.

Another round of cursing told me what my brother thought of my answer to his question.

"Ma is worried sick."

"I know. Is she mad?"

He snorted. "What do you think?"

I took that as a yes. "How mad?"

"Remember when you came home from college with your first tattoo?"

When she'd kicked me out and I had to live with my cousin for the summer. I remembered.

Saying that my strict Irish Catholic mother hadn't approved was an understatement. But her attempt at regulating my behavior had backfired in a big way. I'd gotten two jobs that summer, saved up my money, and in the ultimate act of rebellion, had gotten a full-sleeve tattoo as well as a nose ring.

I bet that one chest tattoo didn't seem so horrible to her after that.

"Yeah," I said.

"Mom's madder than that time," Connor informed me.

I sighed. "Can you please just tell her I'm okay?"

"That's your answer? Tell her you're okay? Do you think that makes disappearing and not answering your phone for days okay? It doesn't. Especially after all that's happened."

He didn't have to remind me about what had happened. I couldn't forget.

As for my mother, she'd get over it. Just like she'd eventually gotten over when I'd gotten my tattoos. She didn't look at me, or talk to me, unless I was wearing long-sleeves that covered them, but she got over it.

"Tell me where you are," he demanded.

"It's safer if you don't know." For everyone. Declan. Me. Them.

The obscenities began again, to the point I had to laugh. That shut Connor up for about two seconds before he asked, "Are you laughing at me?"

"Yes. If Ma heard you, you'd get your mouth washed out with soap."

She'd done it when we were younger and I didn't think that Connor being over thirty now would prevent her from trying to do it again.

"This isn't a joke, Kay."

"I know. And I also know I'm right."

"What the feck are you trying to do, girl?" he asked, the slightest Irish lilt shadowing my older brother's words like it always did when he got emotional.

"Don't get your Irish up, big brother," I teased.

Unlike me, he'd been born in Ireland. He'd even attended a couple of years of school there before my parents immigrated.

"Fuck me. Kayleigh, you have to take this seriously."

I heard the exasperation in his voice. "I am. I'm trying to keep Declan alive."

He drew in a breath loud enough for me to hear it through the phone. "And you'll get yourself killed in the process."

"I'm being careful."

"By not telling your family where you are?"

"Yes. That's part of it."

"That's pure shite. They'll be able to track you. They've got eyes everywhere."

The mob might own a few dirty cops in Boston, but I was sure they didn't here in Mudville. The thought of Carson being on the take was laughable.

But just in case, I hadn't used my real last name when I'd gotten the job here.

Thank goodness one of my cousins and I looked enough alike that I could pass for her in a photo ID. She'd given me her license a few years ago, after she'd turned twenty-one and I was still underage. That way I could drink in the bars at college.

The fact we were both named for my grandmother Kayleigh so we shared the same first name made it even more convenient for me to pretend to be her here in Mudville.

I could safely live here in Mudville as Kayleigh Doyle from Dorchester. Anyone searching for me would be looking for Kayleigh Walsh from Charlestown.

"They can't find me. And why would they be tracking me anyway?" I asked.

"Uh, let me think. Because you've disappeared?" His voice rose.

"I could have gone back to college for all they know."

Connor let out another breath. "You might be the first in our family to go to college, but that doesn't make you the smartest. Not when it comes to them. You can't outplay them. This is their game."

He was wrong. I'd grown up in that world. Just because I was young and a girl, didn't mean I couldn't hear everything said. That I wasn't aware of what was happening. I was. Acutely.

I knew the dangers. I'd seen the results. I'd grieved my grandfather after he'd been killed. I wasn't going to grieve Declan too.

"Kay-bear. Please come home." Connor was desperate. He'd pulled out his old nickname for me.

"No. Not until I find Declan."

"Look. I know how close you two are. I know how much you love him—"

The tears formed as I thought of Declan. My heart physically hurt when I remembered the last time I'd seen him.

"Of course, I love him. He's our brother, Connor. Don't you love him?"

"Yes. Of course—"

He sure wasn't acting like it. It was as if I was the only one trying to find Declan. The only one looking. Definitely the only one who'd turned my whole life upside down and moved to another state to find him.

"Just tell Ma I'm okay. Love you. Bye." I disconnected the call before the huge sob I'd been holding back wheezed out of me.

The phone rang again immediately, but this time I sent Connor's call to voicemail and then set my cell to vibrate. I was sure he'd leave some choice words for me to listen to later. Right now, I couldn't bear it.

He was right. I did love Declan. He was my twin brother. And his being gone felt like someone had carved out half my heart.

I wouldn't feel whole again until he was safe.

Even then, I knew things would never be the same. But at least he'd be alive and out of danger.

That would have to be good enough.

CARSON

I was tempted to go directly to the Muddy River Inn after finishing my shift in hopes that Kayleigh was working.

Why I had that impulse, when she'd literally shown me the door last night, I didn't know.

Maybe I was a glutton for punishment. The sheer number of horrible internet dates I'd been on recently proved that.

I guess I should consider myself lucky that I had the library centennial celebration meeting at six, although I'm pretty sure no one had ever felt lucky for having to attend a meeting in Mudville. At least no one with any sense. Or a life. But for tonight, it saved me from my own bad decisions. I didn't have time to stalk her at work.

Sighing, I drove directly to the library where I'd been last night to check the doors were locked.

I'd been there again this morning too. After they'd opened for the day, I did a sweep of the interior to determine if the possible intruder, if there indeed was one, had left any clues behind.

The small library looked radically different this evening from how it looked during the day.

This morning, the place had been empty, save for one volunteer behind the desk and Alice Mudd, who was there returning some hardcovers and picking out new ones.

Tonight, it was standing room only. The long wooden table was circled by folding chairs two rows deep and even that wasn't enough.

As one of the youngest attendees, as well as a man and a public servant, I remained standing to let the octogenarians have the chairs. It would also make for a quicker escape when this thing was finally over.

Fingers crossed that wasn't too late.

I had to think if there were this many people volunteering to help, why had the ladies all pursued me so relentlessly? Did they really need me here in addition to all the others?

At least I wasn't alone in my misery. As I glanced around, I saw Stone Morgan seated at the head of the table.

I'd bet he was regretting that run for mayor now. There was no getting out of any town meetings anymore for him in his new position of authority in Mudville.

But aside from the two of us, and Roger, the rest of the room's occupants were females. All of them of the more senior variety.

Indicating the empty chair next to him, Stone waved me over, drawing me farther into the room where there'd be no hope of an early escape.

In spite of that, I complied and moved closer, but only so I could explain. "I was leaving the chair open in case someone else needed it."

He dismissed my offer with the flick of one suntanned wrist. "No. It's fine. Everybody's here who's supposed to be, as far as I know."

"Harper's not coming?" I asked.

He let out a low grumble and shot me a glance tinged with misery. "No. She's not coming."

"Really? Is everything okay?" I asked, surprised his author girlfriend—actually, fiancée now—wouldn't be here to support the library in her own town.

"We don't talk about the library with Harper," Stone explained with caution in his tone.

When I frowned, he leaned closer and motioned me to do the same.

"They don't shelve any romance novels here and the board refused to change that when she offered to donate hers," he whispered.

"Gotcha. So are Agnes, Red and Bethany all sitting out too in solidarity?" I asked, noticing the absence of the women in Harper's circle of friends and relations.

"Yeah. It's a whole thing." He shook his head. "I'm

only allowed to be here because it's part of my official duties."

I nodded, trying not to chuckle at Stone's tenuous situation.

No doubt it was a delicate dance and he was doing his best to not add fuel to the fire that was Harper on a rampage.

But we weren't here to talk about Stone's girl. We were here to discuss the library's centennial celebration and then get me the hell out of this meeting at a decent hour.

Glancing pointedly at the watch on my wrist, I said to Stone, "So if everybody's here, you wanna get this thing started?"

Stone drew in a breath and let it out. "That would be a good idea. Except I'm not in charge."

I followed his line of sight when it landed on Alice Mudd and Margaret Trout.

The two ladies were deep in conversation with none other than Mary Brimley, who could talk until the sun came up about everything and anything, or nothing at all.

And wedged in between Margaret and Mary was Roger, looking overwhelmed and helpless.

Immediately, I understood Stone's sigh. We were going to be here all night if this chatter kept up.

"I'll handle this," I offered, still holding out the vain hope I'd get out of here with enough time to swing by the MRI and see if Kayleigh might be still working.

Stone snorted. "Be my guest. Alice and Margaret are officially the co-chairs…"

He let the sentence trail off, but I knew what he meant. Official chairman of the committee or not, everyone in this room was going to have something to say.

Relying on my most authoritative tone, I said, "Ladies. Do you want to get started?"

"Yes. We have so much to discuss." Alice nodded.

"And we're so glad you're going to be involved, Carson," Margaret said.

"They keep saying that," I mumbled.

Stone sniffed out a laugh. "Be afraid, man. Be very afraid."

"Stone. Do you have something to add?" Alice asked, her pale blue gaze pinning my cohort.

Uh oh. Busted.

He'd said it beneath his breath, but somehow the oldest woman in town managed to hear Stone's murmur from the other end of the table.

Stone shook his head. "No, ma'am. Proceed. We're all anxious to hear your plans."

He flashed her the trademark Morgan smile. The one that had won the three brothers all the girls back in high school and still worked just as well on adult women.

The smile that had no doubt played a part in me losing any chance with Red to Cash Morgan.

"Good. Because we're so excited to tell you."

Margaret clapped her hands together. "So, here's what we're thinking—"

"Bachelor auction," Alice said, cutting Margaret off and earning her a glare from her co-chair.

"Bachelor auction?" I swallowed hard, hoping I'd heard her wrong.

"Yes. Isn't it fabulous?" Mary said, clapping her hands together.

No. It wasn't fabulous at all.

Stone sent me a worried glance, letting me know I wasn't alone in my concern.

"So, uh, where will you get all these bachelors willing to be auctioned off?" Stone asked the question I had been afraid to.

"Why, right here in Mudville, of course," Alice said.

"Carson. Carter. John Callahan." Mary ticked off the names on her fingers.

"And anyone else we can think of," Margaret added.

"Stone, you and Cashel can be in it too. Your brother Boone is out, of course, since he's gotten married," Alice continued.

Stone's eyes popped wide, while I was still absorbing how my name had headed the list.

"Um. I can't be in your bachelor auction. I'm engaged to Harper," Stone pointed out.

I noticed Stone wasn't also defending his brother by saying Cash couldn't be auctioned off because he was in a serious relationship with Red.

Apparently, it was every man for himself in this situation.

"He does have a point there. Engaged men should be excluded," Roger said, the voice of reason amid the ladies.

Easy for him to be so calm. He was married so he was safe.

"Ooo. Michael Timmerman is back from the Army," Mary suggested. "He's perfect for this."

I wasn't sure Michael Timmerman would think so. Not that the ladies seemed to care what their victims, or rather bachelors, thought. But Jesus, Michael had lost a foot in combat. Hadn't he sacrificed enough?

"Michael's father is a widower, so technically he's a bachelor too," Mary pointed out. "We should recruit them both."

Stone's brows rose at that suggestion. I had to agree.

Old man Timmerman, the man who'd demanded an in-person apology when one of the shelter dogs had shit on his lawn, was not the kind of personality I imagined taking kindly to being sold at a bachelor auction.

The ladies obviously didn't share my assessment. They all nodded as Margaret added the two new names to the list in her notebook.

"I think we should have more older bachelors for the senior ladies. Such as Buck, for example." Alice grinned, reminding me she and old Buck had started spending a noticeable amount of time together over the past couple of years.

My mind shot briefly to wondering if they were doing more than hanging out before I shoved that thought far away.

The concept of still having sex when I was ninety sounded good in theory, until I actually pictured them doing it. Then, I wasn't so sure.

All I knew was that I didn't want the image of Alice and Buck together like that in my head. Nor did I want to think about what Alice might want to do with Buck if she won him at the auction.

"Don't forget Jeb," Roger added, throwing yet another one of Mudville's single male citizens under the bus.

"Yes." Margaret nodded in agreement. "Stone, you can tell Jeb when he comes to work in the morning."

"Uh, okay." Stone's relief over being excluded from the bachelor roster was short lived.

He looked less than thrilled at the prospect of breaking the news about the auction to one of Morgan Farm's employees. Particularly old Jeb, a farmer from way back who took no shit and told it like it was.

Jeb was barely social on a good day. And I couldn't imagine he would consider the auction *a good day*.

Five minutes into this meeting and I was already dreading this event with every fiber of my being. What other horrors were on the agenda?

I was afraid to ask. I did anyway. Better to know now...

"So besides the bachelor auction, what else do you have in mind for the centennial celebration?"

"An evening social," Margaret announced. "With a band so there will be dancing, of course."

"We thought the evening event will be the perfect place for our bachelors to accompany their new owners, so to speak." Alice tittered behind her hand.

Phew. That news was a relief actually.

Of all the possible scenarios, being able to fulfill my bachelor duties with a single evening event, in public and in the company of my fellow bachelors, was probably the best I could have hoped for. Much better than a one-on-one date.

And if Kayleigh were to bid on me... Yeah, sure. I could keep dreaming about that.

"Don't forget the bake sale," Mary added, bringing my attention off impossible fantasies and back to the meeting. "I'll make my signature cake."

Make was pushing it. Everyone in town knew Mary's cake was a store-bought pound cake that she sliced in half and filled with raspberry jam, also store-bought, then topped with non-dairy whipped topping.

She'd dropped one off at the Sheriff's department once. It was good. Just not homemade, which among the older females of Mudville, was considered a sin.

I didn't miss the glance that passed between Alice

and Margaret before Alice said, "I'm sure everyone would love that."

"Yes. I'm sure," Margaret agreed, although I could hear the sarcasm in her tone.

I almost let out a laugh. If this were a television show, and not my life, it would all be pretty funny.

Pressing his lips together, Stone said, "It sounds like you've got everything all planned. Good job." He pushed his chair back from the table. "Let me know what I can do."

"Oh, don't worry. We have a task list." Margaret opened the very fat folder in front of her and glanced up at Stone. "Do you have a paper and pen? You're going to want to take notes."

"Good try," I murmured as soft as humanly possible.

Stone's only reply was a low grunt before he said, "Let me see if there's paper and pens on the desk." Standing, he glanced back at me. "I'll get you some too."

"Great. Thanks."

It seemed there was a whole lot of sarcasm going around tonight.

8

KAYLEIGH

There was something happening at the library. I arrived just about sunset, but the building was all lit up and there were cars parked in the lot and along the curb.

After spending the whole night in my car watching for Declan last night, and being disappointed, I was tired and cranky at the realization that there was no way he was coming back here tonight. Or anytime soon. Not with all these people inside.

It was going to be another long night. Followed by another long day of work behind the bar with not enough sleep.

Thank goodness my shift didn't start until eleven each morning. But still, the handful of hours of sleep I'd gotten between sunrise and work hadn't been enough.

I couldn't keep up this pace.

If I nodded off while sitting in the car and missed him, I'd never forgive myself.

Maybe I could figure out a way to install a camera. That way it would catch anyone coming or going, whether I was here or not.

It was a good idea and I'd see about implementing it tomorrow. But for tonight, I was stuck here. I eyed the building one more time and, scowling, slumped down low in the seat.

I must have dozed. The next thing I was aware of was a knock on the window.

It startled me awake, besides scaring the hell out of me.

One panicked glance at the side window revealed Carson, bent over and motioning for me to roll down the window.

Seeing no other choice, I lowered the glass. "Uh, hey."

"What are you doing here?" he asked.

"I was seeing if the diner was still open. I was hungry. But I guess I fell asleep." Thank goodness the diner was just down the block, within sight, so the story seemed plausible enough.

"You fell asleep in the car? You must be really tired."

I jumped on that and nodded. "I am. I didn't sleep so great last night."

"I'm sorry. Is there anything I can do?" Carson asked.

Stop asking questions... And looking so damn good.

"No. Thanks. I just have to get used to the new place, I guess."

"Yeah. I guess." He nodded.

He looked like he was about to say something else when I heard, "Deputy!"

I didn't miss the cuss he mumbled under his breath before he straightened and turned toward the woman who'd come rushing up the sidewalk to meet him where he still stood next to my car.

"Deputy—Oh, hello." Her gaze zeroed in on me. "I'm Mary Brimley."

"Uh, hi." The last thing I wanted to do was introduce myself to this woman or have a conversation with her.

While I was figuring out how to avoid it, Carson said, "Mary, this is Kayleigh. She just started working at the MRI."

"Oh. How long ago? I was there just last week and I didn't see you."

"I only started a few days ago," I answered.

"Did you move from the city? I detect some slight accent."

I knew it would be only a matter of time before my sounding like I was from Boston slipped out. I didn't have nearly as much of an accent as some, and at times I could convince myself I didn't have any at all, but obviously I was wrong.

Darn it. I was braced for questions from Carson

but I wasn't prepared for questions from this old lady here, tonight. And this woman beat out professional law enforcement as far as interrogations went.

"Um, yeah," I agreed with her guess.

"Oh. I know lots of people who live in New York. What borough are you from?"

"Uh, all over. I moved around a lot." I glanced at Carson, knowing I had to get out of here before I dug my hole of lies any deeper. "I'm going to head home. It's late."

"Where are you living?" she asked.

Jeez. This woman was nosy.

"Laney hooked her up with a room above the bar," Carson answered for me.

"Well, then, you need to hear what's happening. The Holbrooks—you'll remember their daughter Meghan from school, Carson. I believe she graduated with you. Or maybe it was a year before you. Yes, because I remember she turned sixteen and was driving before you were. Anyway, they live not too far from the Muddy River Inn down that end of Main Street and Meghan has been doing the laundry, because her mother hasn't been feeling well. I think it's cancer, poor thing. She looks terrible, but she hasn't confided that to anyone so don't tell her I said anything. She's alone so much. Her husband works full time over in Greene at Raymond Industries. He travels a lot, all over. In fact, he spends a lot of time in the city," the woman turned to me, as if that information would have me jumping up and saying that I knew this guy.

Yeah. Sure.

"Anyway, Meghan has been spending more time at home with her mother and helping her take care of the house while Mr. Holbrook is away. And Meghan was getting the laundry down from on the line outside because, on top of everything, their dryer broke. But it's been so nice lately, I always hang my laundry out to dry in this weather. I really only use my dryer during the cold weather. Especially for things like blankets. I'd rather hang them outside on the line in the sun when I can. They smell so nice when they're dried outside. Anyway, Mrs. Holbrook swears that when Meghan brought the laundry inside, items were *missing*." Her eyes widened as she emphasized the final word.

For the first time since this woman's eternally long and convoluted story began, I perked up and started to listen.

Clothes missing off a wash line... *Declan*.

"What items were missing? Did she say?" I asked, which had Carson looking at me like I was nuts.

I guess I couldn't blame him for being surprised I'd asked a follow-up question. Most likely he didn't want me to prompt another long diatribe from this woman now that she'd finally stopped talking long enough to take a breath.

"She didn't say. I'm assuming she hasn't said

anything to you yet, Carson, since you didn't mention it at the meeting."

"Well, the meeting was about the library event so…" He let the sentence trail off.

The woman continued as if he hadn't spoken. "I'm sure Meghan will be calling you. Or at least I hope she will. I know there can't be all that much value in what was taken but something like this should be officially recorded. In case it happens again. You know—"

"I agree," Carson cut off whatever else she had to say.

Figuring she had more opinions than facts, I wasn't too upset by that. I'd already gotten the most important information anyway.

Was it possible Declan had grabbed some clothes? It would make sense.

"First thing in the morning I'll check the call logs. If she hasn't filed a report yet, I'll stop by the Holbrook house and take a statement personally," Carson offered.

"Good. Good. That will help. Since it's probably hard for Mrs. Holbrook to get around. And I'm not sure if Meghan is still working as a sub at the school or just taking care of her mother at this point—"

"Oh. Look." Carson glanced at the parking lot. "It looks like Alice and Margaret are still busy talking over there. We should probably make sure they both get into their cars safely."

"Alice really shouldn't be driving at night at her

age. I offered to pick her up and drop her off but she said no. Carson, you really should tell her she shouldn't drive—"

"I think that might sound better coming from you, Mary, rather than me since I work for the sheriff's department. Less official coming from a friend, you know? Maybe you can convince her to get going before it gets any later?" Carson asked smoothly.

"You're right. I'll go tell her." She leaned down and said, "Nice meeting you. Maybe I'll stop by the MRI and see you. What hours do you work?"

Christ. That was the last thing I wanted.

"Um, pretty much every day," I answered. There was no getting around the truth.

"I'll be seeing you, then. Good night, Carson."

"Night," he said with hope in his voice.

Finally, the woman hustled away, making a beeline toward the two other women still talking by the library.

Carson blew out a loud breath. I resisted the urge to do the same.

"Who the hell was that?" I asked.

He sniffed out a short laugh. "Mary Brimley, unofficial town information coordinator."

I shook my head, not sure what to do with that information, except try to avoid future encounters with her. I made do with, "She has a lot to say."

Carson made a sound of agreement. "That is an understatement." He blew out another breath and focused back on me. "Did you get something to eat? I'll go in with you. I wouldn't mind grabbing a bite."

Another time, another place, I would have loved that. Not now. My surveillance was shot as long as Carson was here.

I needed him to go home and the best way I could figure to do that would be to pretend to go home myself and hope he'd do the same. Then I could circle back and wait for Declan.

Missing laundry. The evidence supporting my theory that he was hiding out here in Mudville somewhere was starting to build.

Was he nearby? God, I hoped so.

Meanwhile, Carson was still waiting for an answer. "I, uh, ate. Thanks. I think I'm going to head home and get to bed early."

"I think that's a good idea." His gaze focused on mine too intently for too long, as if he could see right through my lie. Finally he said, "Home safe. I don't want you falling asleep at the wheel."

He really was such a boy scout.

"Yes, deputy." I smiled, and this time it wasn't even fake.

CARSON

I wanted to assume Mary Brimley was wrong. That there wasn't a thief in Mudville stealing laundry off clotheslines. But when Mrs. Holbrook gave me a definitive list of what was missing, it was less and less easy to dismiss Mary's story as a fantasy.

Glancing down at my notebook, I read the list back to her. "One blanket, a men's short-sleeve T-shirt, underwear and socks. And a small cooler that was on the back porch. Is that right?"

"Yes." She dipped her head as I eyed her pale complexion more closely, wondering if the poor woman might actually be sick. "I know it sounds crazy."

I shook my head. "Not at all."

If someone was hiding out, in the woods or in one of the empty buildings in town, those were the exact things they'd need.

It wouldn't be the first time we had a squatter in town helping himself to things here and there. Last time it was a foster care runaway. The boy the Morgans had since taken in.

I could only hope the perpetrator was just as innocent—and just as easily dealt with—this time.

"And were these things taken in broad daylight?" I asked.

That was the only thing that didn't feel right. At least, it didn't seem smart.

She shook her head. "No. At night. I'd hung the laundry out in the afternoon, but I just couldn't get it back in before dark. I've been tired lately…"

That supported what Mary had said.

Not to embarrass the woman for not being able to get the laundry inside before dark, I just nodded and said, "So you noticed in the morning."

"Yes. Meghan came in the morning and when she brought it in for me to fold, I noticed my husband's things missing, along with the blanket."

"And you're sure all these things you listed as missing were actually on the clothesline when you hung the laundry?" I asked.

My life as law enforcement was definitely not anything like the crime dramas on television.

Instead of murders and mayhem, my day consisted of libraries and laundry. But still, my job was to make sure the citizens of Mudville felt safe and happy, so here I was.

"Definitely. It was my husband's favorite T-shirt or I might not have noticed. Then, once I realized that one item was missing, I counted the socks and underwear. He'd just come home from a business trip so I know for a fact there were three pairs of each in that load of laundry from his suitcase because he was gone for three days. But Meghan only brought in one pair of underwear and two pairs of socks from the wash line."

I believed her. Unlike Roger, who couldn't be sure the door to the library had been locked or not, this woman seemed to have intimate knowledge of her family's dirty laundry.

Funny. Most of the people in this town were more worried about dirty laundry of another variety. But Mrs. Holbrook was like the drill sergeant of dirty shirts. The warden of wash day.

I forced myself to stop being so punny in my mind. Mrs. Holbrook looked about to drop.

We'd been standing in the sun in her yard for a while. Sick or not sick, she needed to get inside. I could see her fading.

I flipped my notebook shut. "I'll file a report so we have a record and get a copy to you. I'll also check with the neighbors to see if any security cameras caught anything or if they remember seeing or hearing someone. If you could let me know if anything else goes missing, or if you realize anything else is gone, I'd appreciate it."

"I definitely will. Thank you."

"Thank you." I tipped my head. "Have a good day, Mrs. Holbrook."

With one more glance at the sheen of sweat forming on her forehead, I turned to go.

Maybe when I talked to the neighbors, I'd drop a hint that she was alone a lot when her husband traveled and perhaps they could keep an eye out for her in case she needed anything. There wasn't much else I could do.

By the time I finished with the neighbors, it was past lunch time and I was starving.

I could have grabbed something at the diner. But instead, I found myself heading for the Muddy River Inn.

That choice had less to do with food and more to do with the hot brunette I spotted behind the bar the moment my eyes adjusted to the dim interior.

"Hey." I smiled as I slid onto a barstool.

"Hi. Finished with work for the day?" she asked.

"Sadly, no. Just a late lunch break then I have to get back."

"So then, no beer?" she guessed.

"No beer." I agreed. "Seltzer water, please."

"Sure thing. I'll even throw a lime in it for you."

"Thanks. That would be nice."

Friendly banter. This was good. But our conversation was also all business, which wasn't what

I wanted from her even though I was a customer here at the moment.

"So, any updates on the case of the missing laundry?" she asked as she planted a glass in front of me.

I laughed at the title she'd given my case. "Right? It does feel like a case for Nancy Drew."

Her focus remained pinned on me as she asked, "Were there actually things missing?"

"As far as Mrs. Holbrook is concerned, yes."

"Like what?" she asked. "What kind of things were taken?"

Her interest was odd, but I was willing to take anything I could get from this woman.

"A cooler. Clothes. A blanket," I answered.

"Men's clothes?" Watching my face, she couldn't have missed my brows rise before she added, "Or women's?"

"Her husband's," I answered. "Why?"

"No reason. Just bored. This is the most excitement I've seen in this town since I moved here. Well, besides the case of the library door."

Her short laugh sounded a bit forced.

"Hey. Did you ever figure out if there was someone in the library?" she asked.

I watched her more closely as I chose my words carefully. "No. Not yet."

I was starting to feel less flattered at her curiosity

about my job. Instead, a niggling of suspicion tugged at me over her interest in Mudville's latest petty crime.

But why was I feeling suspicious?

Maybe because she had opportunity—she had been in Mudville during the timeline for both crimes.

And she had means—she had a car. All it would take was her driving into the village both nights.

I had found her sitting outside the diner last night. The night after the Holbrook incident.

But why would she steal men's clothes and a blanket off a wash line in the middle of the night? Or break into the library but take nothing?

She had a place to live. She had plenty of clothes as far as I could see. So there was no reason for her to take anything. And there was no evidence that she had.

Sad that I had to remind myself of the three aspects necessary for a person to become a suspect from my criminal justice courses in college—opportunity, means and motive.

Kayleigh was obviously missing the key one —motive.

What the hell was wrong with me? Suspecting Kayleigh. It was nuts. She probably was just bored, like she'd said. That was why she was interested.

I smiled. "I'll be sure to let you know when I crack the case, Bess."

She frowned. "Bess?"

"Nancy Drew's sidekick," I offered up. "From the books. And the television show..."

Great. Now I really looked like the geek I was.

Worse, I was beginning to feel like a loser. A loser who'd had to resort to reading the Nancy Drew books in my grandmother's bookcase the year of the flood.

In my defense, the storm had knocked out the cable TV. It was raining like hell and the streets were flooded. Going outside was out of the question. So books it was. And the selection had been old Nancy Drews or Harlequin romance novels.

But that didn't excuse the fact I'd actually watched a few episodes of that damn television show. I seriously needed to get a life. And to do that I needed to stop being suspicious of the only girl in town I was interested in.

And I should probably try to keep from looking like the biggest nerd on the planet in front of her and not talk about Nancy Drew anymore too.

Lesson learned.

KAYLEIGH

"Hey. Are you feeling all right?" Laney asked when I went into the kitchen to grab an order.

"Yeah. Fine. Why?" I asked, picking up the hamburger platter.

"You look tired. And maybe a little pale."

"I'm Irish. Pale or sunburned to a crisp are the only two options for me." I laughed, hoping the joke would end this conversation.

Finally, Laney nodded. "Okay. Don't forget to grab the ketchup."

She tipped her chin toward the bottles lined up on the counter.

"Got it. Thanks." I scooped up a bottle and pushed the swinging door with my shoulder.

Laney wasn't wrong. I needed to get more sleep. Obviously, it was starting to show.

But Carson's information earlier today that it had been men's clothing stolen had lifted my hopes yet again. Which made me want to keep looking for Declan tonight.

The emotional roller coaster I was on, as well as the nights spent not sleeping while I searched for Declan, was starting to wear on me. And people were starting to notice.

Tonight, I really should try to find a Walmart or someplace like that after work. Maybe there I could get an outdoor camera.

That way, all I would have to do was hide it somewhere where it would get a view of the library and Main Street. Then, I could get a good night's sleep, wake up early, check the camera and see if Declan had been there.

If he had, tomorrow night I'd sit there until he came again.

If he hadn't— I didn't really have a plan for if he wasn't sleeping in the library. Or if he had been that one time but had moved on to somewhere else.

I suppose I could try some other buildings in town.

He had to be here. Because if he wasn't, I had nowhere else to look.

"I'm telling you, Agnes, something is afoot in this town."

"And what, exactly, do you think is *afoot*, Alice?"

"Thieves! They are living among us. This morning my fresh milk delivery was missing."

The conversation happening between the two old ladies at the table closest to the bar caught my attention immediately.

The third woman at the table, much younger than the other two, said, "Alice, you get fresh milk delivered?"

"Every morning." Alice nodded.

The younger one spun to the other old woman. "Aunt Agnes, why don't we do that?"

Gray brows rose high as she answered, "Because I'm not too old to drive and I can go out and get my own milk when I need it."

"Hey. I'm not too old to drive. I just choose not to," Alice defended.

"And a wise choice it is too, Alice," the one named Agnes said while patting Alice's hand.

"Well, I'm going to look into that fresh milk delivery," the younger one declared.

"Harper, your fiancé owns a farm and a farm stand. His family sells fresh milk. Do you really think it's wise to order it from the competition?" Agnes asked.

Harper pressed her lips together. "Hmm. Maybe Morgan Farm should start delivering their milk—"

Agnes let out a bark of a laugh. "I'm sure Stone will love that idea. Because they don't have enough work over there already, they should start driving around delivering milk too?"

"They could hire someone." Harper pouted.

"Or, how about you just ask him to bring milk home with him?" Agnes suggested.

"That's not as fun." Harper turned to Alice. "Does your milk come in those cute bottles in a metal carrier like in the old days?"

"Yes." Alice nodded.

Harper spun back to Agnes. "See. It won't be the same."

Agnes narrowed her eyes. "You just want this for your Instagram, don't you?"

Harper lifted a shoulder. "It would be a great picture."

Agnes sighed. "Then go over to Alice's house and take a picture of her milk. No one will know the difference."

As Harper looked as if she were considering that idea, Alice raised her hand, as if she were in school. "Can we get back to the fact my milk was stolen, please?"

That tidbit had my heart speeding. Declan could have taken the milk. He'd need food and might be afraid to show his face in a store.

"Did you call the sheriff?" Agnes asked.

"Yes. First thing this morning when I noticed it missing." Alice nodded.

I wondered why Carson hadn't mentioned the milk while he'd been here.

"But I don't trust that John Callahan. He's the one who took my call. He was quite the troublemaker back in school, you know. Not like that nice, sweet boy Carson," Alice continued.

I would have been more amused at her oh so accurate description of Carson, except I was shaking. This was just further evidence that Declan could be hiding out somewhere in this town, pilfering to survive.

The older couple eating in the corner, the Trouts, got up to leave and of course they stopped at the table to say hello to the three women on their way to the door.

It took about two sentences for the conversation to turn back to Alice's missing milk as the man and woman provided all the appropriate anger and commiseration over the theft.

"You know what I'm thinking, Margaret?" Alice asked.

"No. What, Alice?" Margaret Trout asked.

"I think it's time for us to get the Mudville Ladies Amateur Detective Society back together." Alice delivered the proclamation with a definitive nod.

"The what?" Harper looked between the two.

The old man with Margaret had obviously had enough of the conversation. "I'm going to wait in the car."

His wife waved him away. "Fine."

"Harper, who do you think figured out who took those stolen mayoral campaign signs last year?" Alice asked.

"It was the LADS," Margaret added proudly.

Harper's eyes widened. "Oh my God. This is too good. Tell me more about this society."

"Please, Harper, don't encourage them." Agnes shook her head, earning her a scowl from both Alice and Margaret.

"Don't be such a Debbie Downer, Agnes. You can't deny we cracked that case," Alice said.

"And shot a hole in your ceiling when you decided you needed to *start packing* if I remember correctly." Agnes cocked up that brow again at her friend Alice.

Meanwhile, I was too fascinated to even pretend to do my job. Thank goodness the one guy at the bar was still nursing his beer.

"That gun wasn't supposed to be loaded." Alice folded her arms across her chest.

"What other cases have the LADS worked on? When did you form the society? How many ladies are in it?" Harper fired off the questions while digging in her bag and finally emerging with a pen and scrap of paper.

"She's going to put this in a book, you know," Agnes told them.

Alice bobbed her head. "Good. I think the LADS deserve to be memorialized in literature."

"Memorialized?" Margaret asked. "That makes it sound like we're dead."

"Celebrated, then?" Alice suggested.

"Better. So I can start the calls. I still have the member list next to my phone," Margaret offered.

"Good. But where should we meet? And when?" Alice asked.

I saw my chance and leapt into action. Rushing from behind the bar, I grabbed a tray on my way so I could pretend my sole purpose was to clear the corner table.

In reality, I had another plan.

Stopping next to the group, I said, "Why don't you meet right here? I'm sure Laney would love to host the LADS. And if you have your meeting here, then no one member has the burden of cooking or cleaning for everyone."

"I like that idea," Margaret agreed.

"I agree. It is a lot of work having everyone over," Alice said as she looked up at Margaret. "So here, tomorrow?"

Margaret nodded. "Good. That will give us a day to gather information on any other crimes that have happened recently. What time tomorrow?"

"Afternoon? We can't meet too late because we have the meeting for the library centennial tomorrow at six."

"Yes. That's right. Okay. So, three o'clock then?" Margaret asked, for some reason turning to include me in the question.

I nodded. "Good. The lunch crowd will be gone but the after work crowd won't be here yet."

And I would be behind the bar listening to it all.

"Perfect." Alice clapped her hands together. "The Ladies Amateur Detective Society is officially back in business."

As Harper beamed and Agnes shook her head at the prospect, I had to think this couldn't have come at a better time.

I could use all the investigative help I could get.

CARSON

I walked into the Muddy River Inn after work—which apparently had become my new habit ever since Kayleigh had gotten hired.

Inside, I found the oddest sight. The females of Mudville—both young and old—were gathered in a large circle and taking notes.

I took inventory of the cast of characters. Agnes, Harper, Red, Mary Brimley, Alice Mudd, Margaret Trout and Dee Flanders. Even Ruby the hairdresser was there.

It wasn't a card tournament, judging by the setup and the lack of playing cards.

Was this some sort of class? Perhaps some kind of craft lesson? Although there were no art supplies in sight.

Maybe estate planning? But then Dee Flanders, the

town lawyer, would have been leading the discussion and she didn't appear to be.

Frowning, I made my way to the bar where Kayleigh stood and tipped my head in the direction of the odd gathering. "What's going on over there?"

"Them?" she asked.

"Yes, them." Didn't she think this was as odd as I did?

We weren't in the library. Or the community house. Both were places I'd expect to see this group gathered in a large circle.

This was the local dive bar.

Except for the occasional birthday party or high school reunion, the dominant demographic usually skewed toward lone males nursing a drink at the bar.

"That's the Mudville Ladies Amateur Detective Society."

I barely smothered my burst of a laugh. It came out as a snort instead as my gaze cut to the mismatched group before coming back to Kayleigh.

I'd expected her to be controlling her own laugh. Or at least looking as amused as I was by the whole thing, right down to the illustrious name they'd chosen for themselves.

I was having trouble reading her expression. Or understanding it. She looked dead serious.

She didn't seem at all entertained.

On top of that, I could tell she was only half listening to me. Her attention was clearly divided.

She stood at the end of the bar closest to the gathering, technically facing me, but her ear—and her attention—remained trained on the group.

Margaret Trout lifted the pad of paper and angled her head to read through her glasses, "So in addition to the Holbrook clothes and Alice's milk, we've added to the list of crimes the steak missing from the freezer in the Timmerman's garage, as reported by Mary, and the spare change taken from the console in Buck's truck last night, as reported by Alice."

Mary raised her hand. "I checked my own spare fridge in the garage the moment I heard and nothing seemed to have been moved, but I'll have to check my car for change when I get home. We all should check. To make sure it was only Buck's truck and the Timmerman's freezer that was robbed."

"And we should ask our neighbors to check as well and then report back next meeting," Alice suggested.

"If this is really happening widespread throughout the village, I don't think this can wait for the next meeting," Dee Flanders commented, looking concerned.

"We should institute the town-wide phone tree," Margaret said.

"Agreed." Ruby nodded.

"Order up!" Carter's voice came from the kitchen, grabbing my attention and Kayleigh's.

She drew in a breath, looking annoyed at the summons.

Shooting a parting glance at the group, she finally turned toward the kitchen and shoved the swinging door hard before walking through.

Now I was curious. What was happening over at that table seemed like the typical Mudville gossip mill. Small things being blown into overly large proportions.

So what was it that had Kayleigh so intrigued? So annoyed to have to leave her post?

Even more intriguing than Kayleigh's interest in this gathering, was how one member of the group reacted to Kayleigh leaving the bar.

Mary Brimley's gaze tracked Kayleigh's movement out of the room before she leaned forward.

"Not to speak badly, but did anyone notice that this crime wave began just about the same time that the new girl moved to town and started working here?"

Mary had lowered her voice, but not nearly enough.

My eyes narrowed at all I'd overheard. First of all, the term *crime wave* was pushing it, in my opinion. Second, I didn't like Mary accusing Kayleigh without any evidence whatsoever, save for the timing of her arrival.

My kneejerk reaction was to go over there and say exactly that. But I restrained myself, curious to see what else they'd say.

"I did notice that, Mary. And I wondered the same

thing myself," Alice agreed. "I think she needs to be put at the top of the suspect list."

"I heard she's living upstairs here. I wonder if we should ask Laney to search her room for the stolen property," Mary suggested.

"Jesus Christ." Agnes scowled, shooting Mary a glare. "If being in town during this *crime wave*, as you put it, makes her a suspect, then you'd better put all of our names on your list too."

Agnes, bless her, was the lone voice of reason.

"But we've all always been here and there wasn't this kind of petty theft happening. Since the incidences began, the only change in town is her," Margaret Trout pointed out, who'd even dressed the part of a detective.

She could have stepped out of a Sherlock Holmes novel, right down to the tweed jacket, in spite of the heat, as she took notes with what looked like a fountain pen. She even had a couple of Watsons assisting her in the form of Mary and Alice. The only prop missing was a pipe.

"I have to disagree about the lack of prior petty theft in this town before recently," Red said as she shook her head.

Thank goodness she was going to say something, just as I was starting to lose faith in the citizens of Mudville. I knew I could count on Red,

"I own a store," Red continued. "Trust me. I know. Things get stolen all the time."

"That's right. Didn't you have a bunch of things stolen just last year? And wasn't it that foster boy who lives with the Morgans?" Mary Brimley asked.

Without waiting for confirmation she turned and tapped a finger against Margaret's pad of paper.

"He should be added to the list of suspects as well," Mary said.

"Agreed." Alice nodded firmly.

Margaret set pen to paper to add the name.

I watched as things spiraled further downward.

No one questioned why Bart, a former runaway who was now well-cared for on a farm that raised both beef and dairy cattle would want to steal a bottle of milk or a frozen steak—or an old man's T-shirt, underwear and socks.

It made no sense, but the boy's name had been added to the ladies' hit list anyway.

This little club no longer amused me. In fact, it was starting to seem dangerous.

No wonder Kayleigh had been listening so intently. Maybe she'd already made the same determination.

She came out of the kitchen carrying a heavily laden tray with platters of food and headed directly for the ladies' table with it.

Conversation at the table stopped and all eyes turned to her.

The air had palpably thickened. She had to sense they'd been talking about her. Branding her as a suspect in their list of crimes, most of which might not even be crimes at all.

I'd had enough of this amateur law enforcement. As the actual law I couldn't stop them from playing sleuths, but I didn't have to sit here for it.

I planted my hands on the bar and stood as Kayleigh came back, her tray empty now after dropping off the order.

"When do you get out of here today?" I asked.

She glanced at the clock on the wall. "Technically, I'm done. Carter is here already to relieve me. He's in the kitchen with his mom. Why?"

"You want to get out of here?"

She glanced at the table, packed shoulder-to-shoulder with the ridiculous club's members.

"Forget about them." I scowled. "They're going to sit here all day and probably leave you a buck each for a tip, if you're lucky."

Still, she hesitated. Meanwhile, a couple of the ladies in question kept shooting glances our way, as if they were waiting for me to arrest Kayleigh or bring her in for questioning or something.

Based on what? The fact she was new in town?

Annoyed, angry, and mostly just plain disappointed in the people of my town, I reached out and touched her arm. "Trust me. You don't want to be here."

She glanced at them one last time then sighed. "I'll tell Carter I'm leaving."

Happy she agreed, I nodded. "I'll be waiting."

"And where are we going?" she asked.

"Anywhere away from here." I scowled.

She sniffed out a laugh. "That sounds pretty good actually."

I had to agree.

KAYLEIGH

Two dates with Carson in one week. If I could call ice cream cones along the river a date. Which actually, I would.

His suggestion was as sweet and unexpected as the man himself.

Unfortunately, I should be concentrating on finding Declan any way possible instead of cozying up to the drool-worthy deputy.

I could pretend I was still only hanging out with Carson in hopes of hearing something I could use. But that would be a lie. I liked him.

Why did I have to like him?

I didn't have time to like him or anyone else. I had to find more clues. Something to lead me to Declan. Even if it meant enduring hours of listening to the old ladies talk about nothing.

Not to mention that I had to put up with all the nasty, suspicion-laden glances from them.

They looked at me like I was a mass murderer hiding in plain sight among them, just because I was a stranger here in Mudville.

"Hey. You all right?" Carson's question brought my head up.

"Yeah. Sorry."

"You were a million miles away."

"No. Just back at the bar." I forced a smile.

He let out a groan. "Don't worry about the old biddies."

"Old biddies." A laugh escaped me and a genuine smile replaced my fake one.

He smiled too. "It's just one of the many nicknames that Harper, our resident author, has given to the local ladies."

"Wasn't she at that table today?"

"Yeah. She was. Along with one of my friends that I graduated high school with."

"Hmm. They didn't seem to be too opposed to spending time with the old biddies."

"No. I know. I was surprised by that too. Although, you never know. Harper probably is writing a book about lady detectives and was doing research. And Red usually goes where Harper goes. They're best friends." He lifted a shoulder.

A loner like me had trouble wrapping my head

around that. Family stuck together. Yes. But a true best friend? Yeah, I didn't have one of those.

It didn't matter. I didn't have to get to know or like the people in this town. As soon as I found Declan here or got some sort of proof that he was elsewhere, I'd be gone.

My one regret when I left would be Carson.

"Hey. Seriously. Ignore those women. Anyone who wasn't born here gets the same cold shoulder in the beginning. It'll pass."

I laughed. "I'm really not worried."

At least, not about them.

I had plenty else to worry about. Connor tracking me down and dragging me home. Declan still being alive when and if I did find him. Missing the start of the semester for grad school that I'd still have to come up with a way to pay for myself.

Neither of which I'd be able to do if I was still looking for him.

Carson watched me closely, as if evaluating if I was telling the truth, before popping the last bit of cone into his mouth and wiping his hands and mouth with the chocolate-stained napkin.

"I haven't had an ice cream cone in what seems like forever. I'm glad we did this." He smiled.

"Me too." I crunched the final bite of my vanilla-filled cone.

"I suppose we ruined our dinner though," he said.

Spoken like the good boy he was. The bad girl in me didn't agree. "I think ice cream for dinner is perfectly acceptable."

"I guess. But I gotta tell you, when I get hungry again later, I'm eating another dinner," he admitted.

"Spoken like a man."

"Guilty." His gaze met and held mine.

He seemed closer to me. Like he'd leaned in. Or maybe I had. He was going to kiss me. I felt it.

"Ah, dammit." He drew in a breath and glanced at his watch, before focusing on me. "I have to go."

All right. So, no kiss then…

Disappointed, I said, "Oh? Okay."

He moved toward the garbage pail and tossed his napkin inside. "There's another meeting tonight for this committee that I'm on. It starts in like ten minutes at the library and the old biddies aren't going to be happy if I'm late."

"Two meetings in one day for the biddies?" I asked.

He blew out a breath. "If there is one thing that is true about the fine folks of Mudville, it's that they really love their meetings."

"What's this meeting about?" I asked.

The old gossips had provided some interesting details this afternoon, before they'd started to look as if they wanted to mark me as the most likely perpetrator.

Still, I was hopeful. The fact money was missing

from cars, and food from freezers, both taken at night and from houses on Main Street, gave me hope Declan was here.

Carson eyed me reluctantly. "I hate to even tell you."

I lifted a brow. "Now I really want to know."

He sighed. "It's to plan the bachelor auction for a fundraiser during the library's centennial celebration."

"And are you just planning it or are you, you know, going to be… auctioned off?" I could barely get the final words out as I tried not to laugh.

"I know it's funny and if I could get out of it I would, but I can't so yes, I'm going to be auctioned off."

"*Please* tell me the date and time so I can be there. I'll put in for a day off right now to make sure."

He rolled his eyes. "I'll let you know. But for now, I'm sorry. I really do have to cut this short and get to the library."

"No. Don't be sorry. It's fine." It wasn't really but…

"Come on. I'll drop you off on my way." He moved toward the driver's side door.

Two minutes later I was back at the bar, upstairs, alone in my attic room where I'd wait until dark when I could go looking for Declan again.

No Carson. No kiss. Just the taste of vanilla ice cream on my lips and the memory of his rushed goodbye.

It was dangerous to want more. I shouldn't want more from him.

But I did.

Sighing, I set an alarm to wake me up after dark and laid down for a nap until I could go out looking for Declan again.

CARSON

These damn meetings were starting to get to me.

It was bad enough I'd had to cut short what was a really nice evening—if not an actual date—with Kayleigh to get to last night's meeting.

It was even worse that one of the suggestions from Mary Brimley, of all people, had been for the men being auctioned off to be in a swimsuit.

But besides the horror of that idea, which Stone had quickly shot down, it was just all too much for me.

Between being at work from eight until four each day, which I had to do, hanging out at the bar after work for a couple of hours, which I wanted to do to see Kayleigh, and then attending these unnecessarily long and far too often library celebration meetings, I was never home.

I was there basically to sleep, shower and grab a fresh uniform.

The thought that I'd gladly give up sleeping at my own home in exchange for sleeping with Kayleigh in her attic apartment hit me before I was able to focus my attention back on the paperwork in front of me.

For a small town, we seemed to have a lot of paperwork. This recent crime wave, as the ladies liked to call it, accounted for quite a bit of what was piled on the desk in front of me.

The ladies had been coming in all day. They felt it was important that each and every suspected incident they'd talked about at their little detective society meeting be recorded with an official report.

Since it was me and the sheriff alone in the office, guess who got to handle it all. The sheriff might be here, but his office had a door and, as usual, it was closed. That left me, seated at my desk, as the front line—or maybe the sacrificial lamb—every time that door opened.

This old deputy Pete, who didn't willingly talk to me or anyone as far as I could see, usually worked the four to twelve shift. And lately, my other coworker John had been taking way more than his share of third shift, even though he had seniority and could have made me take them if he wanted days instead.

I was starting to realize why John preferred working twelve to eight. I bet the ladies weren't coming in all night to make reports during his shift.

So far today, I'd filed no less than five different reports from all the various people who'd decided loose coins had been stolen out of their unlocked vehicles, although most didn't know how much money had been in the console to begin with.

The only incident I hadn't recorded was the allegedly missing meat from the garage freezer at the Timmerman place. And that was only because Mr. Timmerman refused to come in to report it. That was according to Mary Brimley, his neighbor, who made a special trip just to tell me.

I glanced at the clock on the wall, wishing the time would pass more quickly.

An hour and counting until I could break for lunch…but when I returned, I'd still have half my day to finish.

What had happened to me? I used to love this job. Back when the odd crimes and persistent citizens were spaced out to a few times a month. Unlike today where there had been a steadily revolving door of them.

I hated to admit it or agree with the old biddies, and I really hated the term *crime wave*, but they might be right. Action had picked up lately. But unlike them, I wasn't going to blame the random occurrences on Kayleigh's arrival in town.

That thought was interrupted when the door swung open one more time.

There went all of my hopes that I might make it through the rest of the morning without filing any more reports.

I drew in a breath and braced myself for what would come next.

When Buck walked in instead of one of the town's ladies, it was a relief. Maybe I was worried for nothing.

"I'd like to report a stalker."

Or maybe not...

He'd delivered that very odd announcement in his usual gravelly and grumpy matter-of-fact tone.

Buck wasn't one to cry wolf, which made his statement seem extra odd.

I felt my brows creep up. "A stalker?"

Was Alice getting a little too clingy for old Buck?

I'd had my suspicions about an amorous relationship between them, as funny as that seemed given he was eighty and she was ninety, if they were a day.

Until now, I'd thought it was a mutual attraction, but maybe not. And if that were the case, how the hell was I going to write that up?

I'd never typed the words *unrequited love* in a report before.

"Yeah. There's a car that's been hanging around Main Street. I've seen it a couple of times. But last night, it was parked right in front of my house."

"Any chance you got the license plate number?" I asked.

"I'm lucky I can see to drive over here in the

daylight. You think I can read a license plate on the street in the dark?"

Justly reprimanded, I asked, "Can you describe the vehicle?"

"It was dark."

I smothered a sigh. "Yes, I know it was dark out, but did you maybe see the car pass under a streetlight?"

That earned me a scowl. "That's not what I meant. The *car* was dark. As in a dark color. But I couldn't tell if it was black or navy blue. Or maybe gray."

I nodded. That was at least a little bit helpful. "What kind of car was it?"

"Hell, I don't know. All these cars look alike nowadays. Now, if we were back in the nineteen-sixties, I'd be able to tell you the year, make and model and how many ponies were under the hood."

"I'm sure you could. But this car you saw last night, was it big or small? Boxy in shape? Or more sleek and sporty?"

"It was kind of medium."

"Medium. Okay." I drew in a breath, realizing this was going nowhere.

It would be one more report I had to write up and file that would never do anyone any good. And this was why those cop shows on television weren't even a little bit realistic, with all their clues and suspects. Their car chases and exciting arrests and eventual convictions.

Because most days in small town law enforcement went just like this. Boring and full of dead ends.

"I've got one of those fancy new doorbell things," Buck said, out of the blue.

My eyes widened as I abandoned my useless notes and glanced up. "A doorbell camera?"

"Yeah. My daughter gave it to me for Christmas. She hooked it up. Even put some kind of thing on my phone connected to it, not that I know how to use it. Would that help?" He pulled his cell out of his jeans pocket and held it up for me to see.

"Yes, Buck. That would help." I stood and reached for his phone. "Do you mind if I look?"

"Have at it. Good luck with the damn thing. I'm lucky I can figure out how to make a call with it. I like the old phone in the house. Punch the buttons. It rings. You talk. That's it. No taps or apps or whatever."

As Buck ranted about technology, I scanned the home screen on his cell phone.

I found the camera app easily enough since he didn't have a whole lot on there.

Tapping the icon, I opened it and discovered that his daughter had indeed hooked it up for him. And she'd even gotten him the plan that records and saves video of all movement.

But being on Main Street, the camera caught a lot of motion. Every damn car, truck, person and dog passing by the house got recorded.

I glanced up at him. "About what time did you say you saw this car last night?"

"Let me think." He squinted, narrowing his eyes and glancing up at my ceiling as he thought. "I got up out of my chair in the living room after the local weather on the eleven o'clock news. I remember I was on my way to bed when I looked out the window and saw the car parked along the curb."

I scrolled to the recorded events from approximately eleven o'clock last night and started looking at the video clips recorded after that.

Sure enough, there was a car that pulled up along the curb and just sat there.

"See. It's hard to see what color it is. And it's not really big or small. Just kind of in the middle," Buck pointed out, poking one crooked finger at the screen.

His touching the screen inadvertently made the video clip I'd been studying zoom in, enlarging the image of the parked car. But I didn't need to zoom in.

I didn't need to know the color, or the make or model anymore either. Because by then I'd already recognized the car.

It was Kayleigh's.

14

KAYLEIGH

The pounding on the door intruded on my formerly dreamless sleep, confusing me in my half-awake state.

I'd been out late last night.

Or I guess technically getting home around sunrise counted as being out until early in the morning rather than late at night.

Until Mudville, the only time I'd seen sunrise was when I was rolling in late from a party or bar while at college.

That was much more fun than what I'd been doing lately—cruising Main Street, looking for Declan.

I was more convinced than ever he was here. That he was surviving the best way he could, by taking what he needed at night, and staying out of sight during the day.

If that was what he was doing—only coming out of

hiding to move about town at night—then that was what I had to do as well.

Except for the little detail that I, unlike him, had a day job.

But Laney didn't believe in anyone working seven days a week. So even though I'd told her I didn't mind and could use the money, she'd insisted I have a day off.

Today was that day. My day to sleep in.

So who was disturbing my much needed sleep?

Maybe the other bartender couldn't work and she needed me? I hope not. Even with as much as I needed the money, I needed to get some decent sleep more.

Luckily for me, I'd been too tired to put on pajamas when I'd gotten home. I'd fallen into bed in the yoga pants and T-shirt I'd been wearing for my stake out—for lack of a better term.

How long ago had that been? I glanced at the time on my cell phone.

Six hours ago. Not bad. That was about what I'd been averaging lately.

But I still would have happily slept for another few hours without the interruption—which continued with another round of pounding on the door.

I managed to stand and not fall over, only swaying a little bit as my equilibrium adjusted to being upright and awake. I moved closer to the door.

Still not knowing who it was, I hesitated.

"Kayleigh!"

Carson.

The familiar voice had me reaching for the knob and lock with both hands.

I unlocked the deadbolt and then the regular lock and pulled open the door. Carson stood on the top step, one hand braced on the doorframe while a strange expression clouded his face.

Frowning, I asked, "Is everything okay?"

"I need to talk to you. Can I come in?"

"Sure." I stepped back so he could come inside. He did, closing the door behind him.

Carson, in full uniform, stood awkwardly in the small space that comprised my apartment. That it was dominated mainly by my unmade bed didn't help matters.

His gaze hit on the rumpled covers, before moving back to my own wrinkled clothes and messy hair. I could see the moment realization hit him.

"I woke you. I assumed you'd be working or at least about to start your shift."

I shook my head. "Nope. Day off."

He pressed his lips together. "I'm sorry—"

"It's okay." I waved away his concern but I did still want to know the urgency of this conversation that he'd felt the need to come up to my room to have it. "What's up?"

His lips still in a tight grim line, he finally met my gaze. "There's video of you parked on Main Street for a considerable amount of time last night.

Between approximately eleven-twenty-five and midnight."

Warning bells in my head had my innate instinct kicking in strong.

Certain lessons had been ingrained in me early.

Don't answer any questions unless you had to. If the police brought you in, call a lawyer. Don't admit to anything, ever. It didn't matter if they did have pictures of you doing it. And never ever rat anyone out.

In my neighborhood, I'd grown up trusting in people more than in police. Since some of those people occasionally broke the law to various degrees we all learned young, just from watching the adults around us, how to deal with cops.

The degrees to which laws were broken varied. There were gray areas, as far as most folks were concerned. But not when it came to the unwritten rules of dealing with the law in Charlestown. Those rules were definitely black and white.

Carson might be wearing a deceivingly casual tan colored Mudville deputy sheriff's shirt and pants, not a Boston PD uniform, but he was still the law. The rules applied.

"I'm sorry. Is there a law against parking on Main Street at night?"

His mouth fell open. "Uh. No."

I lifted one shoulder and shook my head, hoping I managed to look confused.

Actually, I was kind of confused. So what if I was parked on Main Street last night? It was a free country. As far as I could see, there weren't any No Parking signs.

Maybe I couldn't sleep and had gone for a drive to look at the stars.

Maybe I was checking on those newborn kittens I'd heard had been born to a stray cat under the porch of the community house. The ones Roger from the library said should be drowned in the river—just one more reason for me to not like the man.

I lifted a brow. "Was that all?"

"Uh, yeah." He looked completely at a loss.

I could imagine why.

The people of Mudville tended to have diarrhea of the mouth. The same question from him delivered to one of the old ladies from the crime fighters committee—or whatever they'd named themselves—would probably be answered for a solid hour.

They'd confess, implicate half the town in that confession and then probably report a few more crimes that hadn't even been on the cops' radar. Just for good measure.

Carson had probably never come upon a girl born and raised in Charlestown. This girl knew my rights and how to keep my mouth shut.

But I also couldn't afford to alienate this man or throw more suspicion on my being here. That would severely hamper my efforts to locate Declan.

That in mind, I smiled. "As long as you're here, want to get something to eat? Now that I'm awake, I'm starving. Maybe the diner? My treat."

His mouth opened again as he paused before answering, "Um. Sure."

"Great. Just let me brush my teeth and change clothes."

That seemed to bring to light for him the reality of just how close these quarters were. The only privacy was in the tiny bathroom, which I could barely turn around in.

He backed a step toward the door. "I'll wait for you outside."

"Okay. I'll be quick," I promised.

"Take your time," he said, already reaching for the knob.

When the door closed behind him, I let my sunny smile drop.

My concern over suddenly being the subject of scrutiny was quickly overshadowed by anger.

I'd done nothing wrong. How dare someone take a video of my car parked on a public street and report it to the sheriff's department.

The anger followed me as I brushed my teeth, washed my face and rolled on some deodorant.

It didn't lessen as I pulled on a fresh T-shirt and then swiped on some lip gloss and cover-up over the dark circles beneath my eyes.

Running my fingers through my hair to fluff away

any flat spots amid my waves from my short sleep, I glanced in the mirror.

This was as good as it was going to get for now with Carson waiting and me in a rush to get outside.

The last thing I wanted was to spend time with a man who'd shown up pounding on my door to interrogate me. But I didn't see how I had any choice.

And, what made me the most angry, was that I had really liked him. A lot. More than I'd liked anyone in —forever.

Why did he have to be the law?

More than that, why did I have to be born into a family with connections to the mob? And why did it seem like we kids were the ones who would have to continue to suffer because of it?

All this chatter in my head—why couldn't my head ever shut up when I needed it too—had me feeling like I was Al Capone by the time I descended the stairs to find Carson. Guilty and about to get nailed for something stupid.

And of course Carson looked even better than when he'd been standing in my room. Then, he'd looked befuddled that I hadn't offered up an immediate explanation or admittance. Now, he leaned confidently against his vehicle, arms folded.

The sun glinted off his dark blond hair. His sunglasses managed to take him from handsome to *hold my panties* hot as the bulging muscles I'd love to lick, and then bite, bulged bigger than usual beneath his short-sleeved uniform shirt.

"Ready?" he asked.

I nodded and tried not to swallow my tongue as I looked at his gorgeousness. "Yup."

I was still mad at him for accusing me of innocently parking on Main Street. I had to remind myself of that as I willingly climbed into his sheriff's vehicle. The act kind of made my skin crawl. It felt too much like being arrested.

But at least he didn't ask any more questions.

Did that mean he'd moved on? Or was he just biding his time? Waiting for me to slip up or give in and reveal something.

If that were the situation, he was going to have a long wait.

In the meantime, perhaps it was time to up my game. I smiled up at him brightly as he slid into the driver's seat after closing the passenger side door for me.

"Thank you, deputy," I said sweetly.

Stone-faced, his only reaction was the slightest cock of one brow before he said, "You're welcome."

15

CARSON

Why was she being so secretive?

That was all I could think as I swung my SUV into the parking lot of the Muddy River Inn and threw it into park, cutting the engine since I intended to walk her upstairs.

"So, two meals together in one day. Breakfast and dinner. People are going to start to talk." Kayleigh smiled sweetly at me.

Maybe a little too sweetly. I pushed away that thought and sniffed out a laugh.

"Breakfast for you was actually lunch for me. But folks around here are going to talk no matter what we do so you might as well not worry about it."

That was the complete truth but I didn't care what they said. I had more than one good reason to ask Kayleigh to dinner tonight after eating with her at the diner earlier today.

Of course, one reason, the main reason, was that I just plain liked spending time with her. At least, I'd been trying to make that the main reason.

The real reason was I needed to find out what she was doing creeping around Main Street in the middle of the night.

I wasn't sure what I thought of her actions, but I knew one thing for certain. If I didn't prove her innocent of all these supposed Mudville crimes, I was afraid the old biddies would brand her as guilty.

Even though I was happy to spend as much time with her as possible for personal reasons, clearing her of any suspicion was the most crucial motivator for date number two today. I needed to knock these doubts about her out of my own head. And, more importantly, out of every head in Mudville.

So when I dropped her off today after our morning meal at the diner, before heading back to work I'd asked her out for dinner.

She'd said yes. Immediately. Enthusiastically even. That had to mean she was perfectly innocent of everything. Right?

Although for the life of me I couldn't figure out what had her parked in front of Buck's place in the middle of the night. Or why she hadn't offered up any explanation.

At least not yet. I had faith she would if I just gave her time.

While I waited, I intended to enjoy our time

together—as much as I could with the shadow of my own damn suspicions as well as those of the Ladies Amateur Detective Society hanging over both of us. And that I remembered the full name of that damn club was proof I was thinking much too much about all this.

"Thank you for today. It was nice to get out instead of sitting upstairs on my day off," she said.

Behind her words I thought I heard sincerity and a bit of loneliness.

All of my doubts and suspicions fled. Replaced by empathy.

She was new. Alone in this town. Living in that little room above a bar.

Even with all the people she saw every day at work, when her shift was over, she was alone. Friendless.

I'd feel lonely too if I hadn't been born and raised here. I knew everyone in town. In addition to knowing everywhere to go and everything to do to keep myself busy when I wasn't working.

All of my knowledge could save her from going back to that room alone for another couple of hours.

I turned in the driver's seat to face her. "Hey. I have an idea. If you don't mind being out with me for a little while longer."

She smiled. "I don't mind one bit."

"Good." I started the engine again and headed toward the drive-in movie theater.

A mile down the road I pulled in front of the now

vacant antique shop directly across from the drive-in's entrance as Kayleigh gasped when the larger than life picture flashed on the screen.

"Is this—an actual drive-in movie?" She turned to look at me.

"It is. Ever been to one?" I asked her.

"No. There aren't too many in—um, the city."

"I imagine not." I smiled as, wide-eyed, she watched the images on the screen.

When I turned on the radio and punched the button preprogrammed to the station that broadcast the sound for the drive-in's movie, her amazement grew ten-fold.

Her gaze shot to the car radio and then back up to the screen. "Wow. That's really cool."

"Yeah. It is." Having grown up here, sometimes I forgot how cool it was.

Seeing it through her eyes reminded me.

"So, they play a double feature every weekend. Two movies with a break in the middle. We can drive in, buy a couple of tickets and park closer if you want. I just wasn't sure you were up for such a late night. Since I kind of woke you up and you didn't get to sleep in on your day off."

"Can we just sit here and watch for a little bit?" she asked.

"Sure." I nodded and couldn't help smiling again as she gazed up at the screen with amazement.

As I watched her watching the movie, I grew more

and more convinced there was no way Kayleigh could have been up to something last night.

Why would she be? And what kind of trouble could she be getting into on Main Street where every house nearby could see her?

It made no sense. Just like how the idea of her stealing milk, or change, or men's clothes or frozen food didn't make any sense either.

There had to be some other explanation and I was going to find it.

And in the meantime, I was going to enjoy my night with Kayleigh.

"There's a snack bar. Want some hot buttered popcorn?"

"Really?" Her eyes brightened.

I laughed. "I'll run across and get it."

"Don't go to any trouble—" she said as I got out.

"No trouble at all." And if I spent some dough at the snack bar I'd feel better about not buying tickets to watch the movie. "Something to drink too? They've got cola and root beer—"

"Root beer."

"You got it." I grinned at her excitement.

Look at me. On an actual date. And a good one at that, after a string of epically horrible ones.

The nagging voice in the back of my brain reminded me I'd asked her out partially because she was a suspect. I told that voice to shut the hell up.

Kayleigh was no more involved in what was

happening around town than I was. Just because there were a few mysteries around here that had yet to be solved didn't prove anything.

But still… I couldn't fathom why she was parked at Buck's. And why she wouldn't answer my question.

Shit. The voice wasn't listening to me.

Fine. The only thing to do was solve these Mudville mysteries and prove my nagging—and incorrect—intuition wrong.

I was going to do exactly that. Then it would be all smooth sailing for Kayleigh and me.

KAYLEIGH

"Kayleigh."

The sound of my name broke through my sleep. Slowly. Softly. Gently. Much nicer and more pleasant than this morning's jarring awakening.

My eyes were closed and, I realized with embarrassment, my mouth open as I dozed in the passenger seat in Carson's car.

I closed my mouth and swiped at my chin to make sure I wasn't drooling. "Sorry. Guess I fell asleep."

He let out a soft chuckle. "Don't be sorry. I can't tell you how many times I've fallen asleep trying to watch the movie. I'm gonna take you home."

"Okay. Thank you. I really did have a good time."

I saw beneath the beam of the streetlight that he shot me a crooked smile as he reached for the key in the ignition. "Me too."

At times like this, when he was sweet and I was

sleepy and vulnerable, it was easy to forget who we both were. Why I was really here in town. The huge Grand Canyon-sized conflict that stood between us.

I could allow myself to forget for a little while, but not for long.

My mind turned to Declan and how it was well past dark. I should be out looking for him.

Even if I did take tonight off from looking for Declan, I really should at least go grab the memory card out of the camera I'd finally gotten around to hiding in a tree by the library. That way I could make sure I didn't miss him.

I shot a glance sideways at Carson next to me.

Or—I could just worry about the trail cam tomorrow.

A wave of guilt hit me. I shouldn't be out enjoying a movie with Carson, even if it was the only fun I'd had since arriving.

I shouldn't even be sleeping, though I needed to. I should be out trying to find Declan.

When Carson flipped on the blinker and slowed to turn into the parking lot about a minute later, I was once again struck by how close we'd been to the bar. I really hadn't seen anything of this town except for about two miles of Main Street and the bar where I lived and worked.

"I can't believe I've been living like a mile from a drive-in and didn't even know it existed."

"Give yourself a break. You haven't been living

here all that long." He cut the engine and glanced at me in the dim interior as he pulled out the key. "I bet there are lots of places you'd enjoy that you haven't seen yet."

I'd bet there were—and I couldn't help but think those places I would enjoy but hadn't seen yet were all hidden beneath Carson's clothes.

He'd changed out of his uniform after work before he'd come to get me in his own vehicle tonight for dinner. He looked good in a tight collared short-sleeved shirt in a sunny yellow that complemented his tanned skin and dark blond hair to perfection. He'd look better without his shirt.

"Walk me upstairs?" I asked before I could think better of it.

I didn't need him to walk me up the single flight of steps to my door. I just needed him—full stop. And even the mess I knew I'd left in the apartment didn't stop me from wanting to drag him up the stairs and inside.

"Of course." He nodded.

He probably would have walked me up anyway—but I didn't want to take any chances he'd say goodnight and drive away. I had other plans for him. For us. For tonight.

The list of pros versus cons was about equal when it came to the idea of sleeping with Carson.

Equal odds were pretty good in my opinion, given how shitty things had been for me and my family and Declan, lately. Hell, I'd take fifty-fifty any day.

Pro. I liked him a lot. I wanted him even more. Make that a double pro.

Con. If we got physical, there was a good chance I'd start to get attached to him. It would hurt like hell when I left here—and there was no doubt I was leaving here. Make that one a big whopping con.

He worked for the sheriff's department—I'd put that in both the pro and the con columns. On one hand, it was risky to hang around with the law. But on the other hand, it was important for me to know what the sheriff's department in this town knew and what they were up to.

See? Fifty-fifty… Until we got to the top step and he leaned in…and kissed me.

The first gentle touch of his lips against mine stole my breath.

It was just a brush of his mouth over mine at first. Quick. Too quick.

I felt him start to pull away until I dragged in a shaky breath.

He must have heard the need in that one sound. Felt how lonely I was and how badly I wanted to be held. Wanted to forget. Because his mouth covered mine again, harder this time in a kiss packed with the intensity of a man who wanted a woman.

His need matched mine. And I was pretty damn needy.

The scales tipped way in favor of the pro column as I pulled back and asked, "Wanna come inside?"

"Yeah," he answered, his voice gruff. "I really do."

Good answer. I managed to get us inside but that was the last thing I did. He closed and locked the door before he turned back to me.

Carson seemed less than the boy scout he'd proven himself to be as he planted a palm on each of my ass cheeks and hoisted me up. As I wrapped my arms and legs around him, he claimed my mouth.

Tongues tangled and parts lower started to tingle from his searing, soul-deep kiss.

"You sure about this?" he asked after pulling away just enough to get the words out.

"Yes," I gasped as I pulled his head back toward mine.

His response was a groan as he walked heavily while still carrying me toward the bed just steps away.

The mattress creaked and the bed frame groaned as the two of us toppled onto the bed.

"This thing going to hold us?" he asked, looking concerned.

"I guess we'll find out," I answered, fisting the fabric of his shirt and pulling his mouth back to mine.

At this point I didn't care if we ended up crashing through the floor to the seating area of the bar below.

That would sure give the old biddies something to talk about. Something other than the crime wave here in Mudville.

His weight on top of me, pressing me into the mattress, felt like a hug. Comforting. The physical contact I'd been missing in my loneliness here. But it was so much more.

It was a prelude. A promise of satisfaction to come. Of how good it would be when he finally plunged inside me. That was all I could think of as his tongue tangled with mine.

When Carson rolled off me and sat on the edge of the bed I was concerned he'd changed his mind and was going to leave until he opened his leather wallet and pulled out a condom.

"Such a boy scout. Always prepared." I smiled.

He tossed the wallet on the nightstand, kicked off his sneakers and then stood.

Hands at the waist of his pants, he had the belt, button and zipper undone and the pants sliding down his legs in seconds. His shirt soon joined the pants on the floor.

He stood in front of me in nothing but underwear that did nothing to hide his hard length. I finally wrestled my eyes up to his face. His eyes were narrowed with desire as his gaze locked on mine.

He let out a snort. "Definitely not a boy scout tonight."

17

CARSON

The sound of the air conditioner chugging away in one of the two windows in the apartment was the first thing I was aware of, followed by the sunlight streaming in.

The sun was up. That meant I needed to get up as well. It was the last thing I wanted to do.

After holding myself in check since meeting Kayleigh, I'd finally given in. Finally let myself go with her. And the result was both not good and at the same time absolutely incredible.

Not good because I could see she worked too hard and slept too little but I'd kept her up half the night anyway.

Anyone could see she was on the edge of exhaustion. But that didn't seem to keep me from loving her until well past midnight. And then waking her up to do it all over again just before dawn, because yeah, being with her was freaking amazing.

Feeling selfish, but still pretty damn good about things, I rolled over and glanced at the clock.

Just that motion woke her next to me in the narrow bed. She groaned. "What time is it?"

"Early. Seven. Go back to sleep," I said as I traced the inked floral design on her arm with one fingertip.

"Good idea, since somebody kept me up half the night." She reached for me, tugging me closer and at that moment I wanted nothing more than to stay.

She sounded soft and sleepy and the last thing I wanted to do was leave, but I was going to have to. "I have to go. I need to get home, change into my uniform and get to the department. You should try to get some more sleep before work."

"I'll be fine."

I leaned in and kissed her, but only briefly. "I know you'll be fine. But try to sleep some more anyway."

"Yes, sir."

A smile twitched my lips. Wide awake Kayleigh was never this compliant. I found I liked sleepy Kayleigh. Hell, who was I kidding. I liked all sides of Kayleigh.

Even the secretive side?

I pushed that errant thought away. It was bad enough I had to leave her bed when all I wanted to do was snuggle under the covers with her in the cool room for another hour or two. Then try to work up a sweat again between the sheets like we had last night.

But it was not to be. I had work today. But I didn't tomorrow. That helped preserve my good mood even as I stood and reached for the clothes scattered around the floor.

Pulling on my shirt, I glanced at her looking too tempting in the bed. "I had a good time."

"That's an understatement, but me too." She smiled sleepily.

"I'll stop by the bar on my lunch break later," I promised.

"I'll be there," she said, and I realized it was hard to remember what it was like before she was here in town. And in my life.

I resisted the urge to tell her I'd also be coming by after my shift. And hoping to do something together tonight. And also planning to sleep here again since I had tomorrow off and we could stay in bed until her shift started.

Things were moving fast. But I'd expect nothing else. With a woman like Kayleigh it felt like full throttle was the way to go. I was fine with it, as long as she was.

I was dressed but still dragging my feet. Delaying the inevitable wouldn't do any good.

I leaned down and kissed her one more time. "See you later."

"Later," she replied.

Sighing with resignation I moved toward the door. "I'll lock up on my way out."

"Okay." She already sounded out of it.

I smiled. Horrible as it was, she was adorable when tired. And it didn't hurt my masculinity to think I'd had a big part in wearing her out.

With that in mind I finally said, "Bye."

"Bye." That was barely a mumble from her face pressed against the pillow.

The image of her carried me home to change, then all the way to the office and through the first half of my day.

It helped that the crime spree seemed to have slowed and I didn't have any more of the ladies coming in to file reports about various missing things.

Things were nice and quiet. A good thing too, since I couldn't focus my mind on anything except thinking about Kayleigh and watching the clock, waiting for the minute I could leave for lunch.

I had it bad for this girl…and I liked it.

Finally, the hands on the old clock on the wall were both straight up. Lunchtime.

"I'm heading to lunch," I called in the general direction of the sheriff's office.

I didn't wait for a response before I was out the door and headed to my vehicle.

Five minutes later I was swinging into the parking lot of the Muddy River Inn with my heart pounding and the adrenaline pumping at the thought of seeing her again.

I strode through the door and was halfway to the bar by the time I had my sunglasses off, only to come to a halting stop when I saw there was no one behind the bar.

That was fine. She could be serving a table. I glanced around the seating area and saw a table in the back with drinks but no food yet.

So she was in the kitchen then.

There was definitely no reason to think she was gone. I mean I guess I could slip outside and see if her car was still here.

Jesus. I was paranoid. There was no reason for her to leave town. And there was really no reason for my sixth sense to be on high alert.

It was silly. The effects of living in the same small town my whole life where people were born, and people died, but they rarely left.

When the kitchen door swung wide and I saw her I blew out whoosh of air.

There she was. My girl. Carrying a tray that looked impossibly big compared to her. I resisted the urge to help her—boundaries—and instead took a seat on one of the old worn barstools where I could catch my breath and try not to chastise myself for being an idiot.

I was doing a good job of it too, when the door at

the front of the bar flung wide and crashed against the wall.

Jeb limped in—which was nothing new. The farmhand was old as dirt and during that long life he'd had countless bones broken and been struck by lightning, more than once if the stories were true.

What was strange was the speed with which he hobbled toward me and the manic expression on his normally passive features.

"Bones," he gasped, his bloodshot gaze on me.

"What?" I asked, confused. Was he drunk? Or having some sort of stroke that made him blurt out random words?

"Bones." He paused to wheeze in a labored breath. "Bones in the pig pen."

That didn't clear a whole lot up. "What do you mean? What kind of bones?"

Was someone killing the farmers' pigs now? Missing milk and spare change was one thing, but livestock was another. That was serious.

As my mind ran through all the possibilities, one more horrible than the next, Jeb's eyes grew impossibly wider. Until finally he said, "Human bones."

I heard a gasp behind me and turned in time to see Kayleigh had frozen in place behind the bar, tray still in her hands, at the appearance of Jed.

Now, pale and wide-eyed, she swayed.

Things seemed to move in slow motion. Still, I

couldn't get to her in time. I watched while the plates crashed to the ground as the tray she held tilted and then dropped.

She reached for the bar but was unable to catch herself before, falling backwards, she went down and her head hit the floor with a sickening thud.

KAYLEIGH

"Kayleigh. Kayleigh."

Someone was shaking my shoulder. And I could smell—bar floor. It was an odor I'd become familiar with when working as a bartender to earn money during college.

As I felt the hard surface beneath me, I realized I'd become even more intimately familiar with the floor of the Muddy River Inn now that I was flat out on my back lying on it.

I'd landed hard. The proof of that was the sore spot on the back of my head. Worse, it was in how my head felt. Rattled. Stunned. Like a bird that had hit a window.

I groaned and pressed my hand to my head.

"She's coming to."

"Thank goodness."

"Why did she pass out?"

"Drunk maybe?"

"Pregnant is my guess."

The sheer number of different voices, in addition to what they were saying about me, was enough to make me want to keep my eyes closed. Except that I had to defend myself.

I dared to open my eyes as I said, "I'm not pregnant. Or drunk."

Being pregnant would require my having had sex in recent memory, which, until about twelve hours ago, I had not.

Even a good Catholic girl like me knew enough about sex to know I wasn't passing out from being pregnant from last night's sex, even if one of Carson's swimmers had managed to make it through the condoms he'd worn both times we'd done it.

I struggled to sit up, if only to defend my honor and prove to the town's people I wasn't hiding a pregnancy or a drinking problem, when I remembered the words that had taken me off my feet.

Human bones in the pig pen.

Jesus. The black began to appear on the edges of my vision again and I felt myself sway.

Laney was suddenly eye-level with me as she squatted down.

She laid her hand on my shoulder. "Don't sit up too fast. Stay there for a bit."

"I'm fine." And even if I weren't, this floor was the

last place I'd want to stay and recuperate. I had to get up. I had to find out what had happened.

Human bones. Declan.

The words echoed in my head as my stomach twisted.

"Let me get her up."

Carson's voice sent a thrill through me, as much as his touch as he wrapped his large strong hands around my midsection and hoisted me up and off the floor.

I made it to my feet and swayed only a little. "Thanks."

"Anytime." There was concern in his eyes, mingled with something else. Confusion, maybe.

I forced out what I'd intended to be a laugh, though I'm not sure I managed it. "Hopefully there won't be another time."

His brow cocked up. "Hopefully. Come on. I'm taking you upstairs."

My first instinct was to fight him. I wanted to be down here. I needed to hear more. Learn whatever I could.

God, what if it were him? Declan's bones.

My mind flashed back to a memory. A conversation I'd overheard years ago. Back when I was young enough I could sit on the floor playing and no one noticed me. They'd talk freely. And I'd listen.

My grandfather, father and uncle were sitting around talking when my uncle said, "Five days. That's all it takes for a single pig to completely devour an average sized adult man. Now, if you got a few pigs, you can cut that time down to a single day."

My father had challenged him by asking where he was going to find a bunch of pigs in Boston.

They'd all laughed. Then the conversation had moved on to other topics. But I'd never forgotten it or the horrible image it had instilled in my young mind.

I needed more information. Maybe I could get it if I let Carson take me upstairs to lay down. Then I could sneak back out after he left. He wouldn't stick around. He was still on duty and there were bones to investigate.

Bones…

The sickening words had me swallowing before I agreed to let him take me up to my apartment.

"Okay," I said to Carson before I glanced at Laney. "Unless—do you need me? Who will watch the bar?"

"I can watch the damn bar like I did for the past twenty-five years. Don't worry about it. Go rest."

I nodded. "Thank you."

I let Carson wrap his hand around my arm. "You feeling okay enough to walk up the stairs with my help?" he asked.

"Yeah." I'd always feel safe with Carson the man. It was Carson the deputy that was making me feel less safe now as a new idea hit me.

What if they weren't Declan's bones? What if Declan had gotten the jump on whoever was tailing him from Boston and he'd killed them and dumped the body in the pig pen?

That scenario made me feel almost, but not quite, as sick as my first guess.

I'd have no problem convincing Carson I was ill and needed to rest now. It wasn't a lie. This was all too much.

I let him lead me up the narrow wooden exterior staircase.

We made it up and inside, but my legs were weak and my head woozy as I lowered myself to the edge of my bed.

"Can I get you anything? Water?" He palmed my face and looked at me with such tenderness, I nearly weakened. Almost asked him to hold me and make me forget all the horrors filling my brain.

Instead, I shook my head. "I have some bottled water in the fridge if I need it." I tipped my head toward the small refrigerator that I used as a night table on one side of the bed. "I think I can manage to get to it without fainting."

"Why did you? Faint, I mean," he asked, still looking at me closely as worry etched his brow.

"*Not* because I'm pregnant," I said.

"I never thought you were. It's just, you went down so fast. And so hard." He ran his hand over the back of my head gently and hissed in air between his teeth when he encountered the small lump I'd already felt on the back of my skull.

As woozy as I was, I still knew I couldn't tell him it was the concept that my brother was either dead or a murderer that had me blacking out. Neither scenario was good. But those bones were the key.

"I don't know. I guess I kind of forgot to eat this morning," I lied.

It sounded like as good an excuse as any. He had left me sleeping. It was believable that I'd slept late and went downstairs to work without eating.

"I can get you some food."

"No. I have food up here. I'll eat. I promise."

As much as I wanted Carson near, I also needed him gone.

Why was he still here? Shouldn't he be investigating those bones?

Did him still being here mean he thought it was a false alarm? Just another old guy in town with an active imagination like library dude?

I forced myself to look at him and ask the question that had my stomach turning. "What was that about—human bones?" I swallowed the acid from my throat.

He sat next to me on the bed and pressed his lips together. "I don't know. I called it in. The sheriff is meeting Jeb over at the farm to check it out until I get over there."

"Could they be…real?" I asked.

The men—the organization—that Declan had been involved with were bad. Killing him and feeding him to the pigs wouldn't be out of the question. In fact, if even half of the things I'd heard about them were true, that would be one of the milder things they'd done.

"Real bones, probably. Human? I have my doubts," Carson continued, reaching out to lay his hand over mine.

"Really?" I asked.

I flipped my hand over so we were palm-to-palm and laced my fingers with his. It felt nice. Almost normal even though my life was anything but.

"Really. It's probably an animal. I mean, it's a farm. It makes sense it's an animal." He gave my hand an encouraging squeeze.

"I hope you're right." I squeezed back.

Carson nodded, keeping my hand in his big warm one. "So do I, Kayleigh. So do I."

I didn't want to let him go, even though I knew I had to. Let him go now, so he could go back to work and I could sneak out.

And let him go later when—for better or worse—things were resolved here one way or another and I went back to Charlestown. Back to my life of riding the line between the criminal world and the world of a law-abiding citizen.

His cell vibrated. With a sigh, he released my hand and stood to be able to free the phone from the pocket of his pants.

He glanced at the screen and then swiped to connect before pressing it to his ear. "Bekker."

There was a moment where all I heard was the

muted garbled voice with no discernable words coming from the person on the other end of the call. But Carson's expression told me more than words.

It went from shock to confusion to concern. That was enough to have me on my feet again. At least I was next to the bed and there was a thick throw rug covering the hardwood floors for me to land on if I passed out again.

Finally, he said, "I'll get right over there." Then he lowered the phone.

"What happened?" I asked, realizing my voice was shaking.

"Petunia's missing," he said with a dark tone of foreboding.

"Oh, no," I said with a suitable amount of concern as my mind spun.

Which one was Petunia? There were so many old ladies. I didn't think I knew all their first names.

More importantly, were those Petunia's bones?

I hated to admit it, but that thought gave me hope. Better poor old Petunia, whoever she was, than Declan.

"I gotta go." Carson pressed the quickest kiss to my forehead. "Get some rest."

"I will," I promised, not intending to do it.

I needed to find out more about those bones.

CARSON

When I arrived at Agnes's house on Main Street, Harper was red-eyed, as if she'd been crying. And Agnes looked like she was doing a good job of fighting back her tears, but I could tell the loss of Petunia had hit her hard.

Meanwhile, as critical as this situation was for Agnes as well as the Mudville High School football team who considered Petunia not just their mascot but their good luck charm, my mind was at the farm.

The sheriff was at the Morgan's place waiting on a forensic team to arrive to take a look at the bones. He'd had to call them in from a police department forty minutes away. Mudville had many things, but with only a thousand or so citizens in our jurisdiction, our own forensic team was not one of them.

Not that I really thought the bones were human, but just the investigation to prove they weren't would be more excitement than I'd seen in months on this job and I would like to be there for it.

I'd get over there eventually. But first, I had to figure out what had happened to Petunia.

"Are you sure she didn't break out of the pen?" I asked, still standing in the driveway.

I knew Agnes gave the pig free rein, letting her in the house. Walking her on a leash through town. The pig was used to doing pretty much what she wanted. Maybe today, she wanted out of the pen.

"I don't see how," Agnes said. "But feel free to investigate for yourself."

"If you don't mind—"

"Not at all." Agnes led me to the carriage house, a sniffling Harper bringing up the rear. "I checked the fencing. It's all intact."

I walked up next to Agnes and stood looking at the pen built into the side of the old carriage house.

"And this gate was closed or open when you discovered her gone?" I asked.

"Closed."

"And latched," Harper added.

"And latched," Agnes agreed, glancing at me. "Harper fed Petunia breakfast so she was concerned that maybe she'd forgotten to latch the gate."

"But I didn't," Harper jumped to say.

"You didn't. It was perfectly secure when I came out to feed her dinner. Just no Petunia inside." Agnes's voice, heavy with emotion, got husky at the end of the sentence.

"Were you home all day?" I asked Agnes.

"No. I went out for a bit and Harper was up in the attic busy writing."

"And did you see Petunia when you got home?"

"I didn't notice if she was in there or not. I came and went by the front door. I walked to do errands in town. I should have looked," Agnes's voice broke as she pressed a hand to her chest.

Harper moved closer to her aunt.

This might not be an exciting assignment, but it was an important one.

"It's okay. We'll find her. I promise. She can't be far," I said.

"Unless someone took her," Harper piped in.

Surprised, I turned to look at her. "You think someone took her?"

She shrugged. "How else could she get out of a closed pen?"

I glanced at Agnes and saw her nod. "It's a possibility, I guess. Wouldn't be the first livestock to go missing around here."

Sadly, that was the absolute truth. But unlike the last instance of runaway, possibly stolen, livestock, this situation was different.

Petunia had been living with Agnes for years. Any controversy about her breaking the law by being here on Main Street—which was not zoned for livestock—had been settled long ago.

Now, the pig was an integral part of the culture of this town.

"Who would take her?" I asked, honestly at a loss.

"Who would take her?" Harper parroted, wide-eyed. "Let's see. The stock auction owner who's still upset he keeps losing his runaway animals. The zoning board who's still pissed Agnes is keeping Petunia in town. One of the fraternities from the college making their pledges take her as a hazing challenge. A rival school stealing the other team's mascot…"

Harper ticked off her many suspects on her fingers. And damned if one or two of her suggestions didn't make sense.

I even wrote them all down, partially to make her and Agnes feel better. Mostly so I felt like I was doing something to help. I had no idea where to start looking for Petunia. Or how to find her.

Unless…

"You have a doorbell camera, right? Did you check that?" I asked, remembering the success I had with Buck's camera.

Harper's face fell. "It was off."

"Off? Why?" I asked.

Now it was Agnes's turn to comfort Harper. "Harper can't concentrate to write if the WiFi is on so sometimes she turns it off when she's working."

"And the camera is hooked to WiFi." I nodded, understanding now.

"That's my fault. But I'm going to do everything I can to find her. I'm going to put it out on my social media right now in case anyone knows anything," Harper said, cell phone already in her hand. "And on the community bulletin board," she added, tapping on the cell as she talked.

Again, I'd been out-thought by a civilian—or maybe just taught a lesson about how law enforcement operated during the age of social media.

That was something I hadn't learned from the current sheriff, a man firmly in the Boomer generation who still had a phone with a dial and a cord in his office.

While I was considering that, a big old Cadillac crept slowly down Agnes's driveway.

I could barely see the shrunken ninety-year-old behind the wheel, but I recognized the vehicle as belonging to Alice Mudd.

Thank goodness she didn't live too far away since whether she should be driving was questionable in my mind.

"And here they come," Agnes mumbled.

I sent her a questioning look, as Alice swung the big door wide and trotted over, surprisingly spry for her age.

"Goodness, Agnes. I just heard about poor Petunia. But don't worry. I set the phone chain in motion. The

Ladies Amateur Detective Society is on the case. We'll get her back."

Agnes nodded. "Thank you, Alice. But Carson's on it."

"Me too," Harper announced. "I'm posting it on social."

"Don't forget to put it on the LADS Facebook page too."

"I won't," Harper assured.

At the same time, Mary Brimley hurried down the driveway.

"I'm here to help. Ooo, my word. Look at your lavender. It's lovely this year." Mary bent to run her hands over the purple blooms, sniffed her fingertips, then straightened. "Tell me what to do to help poor Petunia."

Agnes shot me a sideways look, then once Mary got within hearing range said, "Thanks, Mary. But Carson's here. I think we're good."

"Nonsense. You can't have too many eyes and ears on the streets in these situations," Alice said.

"Do you think we need to call an emergency meeting of the LADS?" Mary asked.

"It couldn't hurt," Alice agreed.

Christ. I had to get out of here before I ended up stuck in another damn meeting.

I flipped my notebook shut. "I'm going to get right on this."

"Wait!" Harper held up one hand, palm facing me. "I've got something."

"What do you mean you got something?" I frowned.

"The Warriors just posted, bragging they are, and I quote, *going to cook the Hogs' bacon* at the next football game."

"Good Lord. They're going to kill her." Alice clutched her chest.

"Oh my." Mary's eyes widened, her hand coming up to cover her mouth that was open in horror.

Agnes shook her head, jaw set. "Over my dead body."

I shook my head. "I'm not sure that's what they mean. It just sounds like the usual trash talk between rival teams to me."

As the quarterback of the Hogs back in my high school days, I'd been the recipient of plenty of it personally.

Times might have changed. Trash talk might have gone from the sidelines to cell phones, but it couldn't be that different.

And I seriously doubted the other team was up for slaughtering a pig…although this was farm country.

Shit.

Agnes set off with a determined stride, skirting around the herb garden in her path toward the house.

"Aunt Agnes, where are you going?" Harper asked.

"To get the shotgun."

"Agnes. No. I'm sure that's not necessary." I took a step after her.

She didn't turn around as she said, "Carson, you're either coming with me or arresting me. You can decide which while I load the gun."

Oh, man. This had unraveled quickly.

20

KAYLEIGH

Since I couldn't just drive up the Morgan's driveway and ask the sheriff how things were going with the bone investigation, I'd had to park down the road and walk.

Luckily it was corn season, and apparently the Morgans grew a lot of it. I skirted along the edge of the fields, then ducked in between the rows, using the tall stalks for cover.

Finally, I got close enough that from my hidden position I could see and hear the group.

The old guy who'd run into the bar to report the bones was there. I also recognized the three Morgan brothers. They stopped in often enough to eat or drink at the bar.

There was also a slightly older couple that I assumed were Morgan family members, judging by their look of concern and casual work clothes.

I didn't know the older man. But he was wearing a uniform that looked a lot like the one Carson wore. It was an easy assumption to make that he was the sheriff, judging by his age. And he had more patches and stuff on his shirt than Carson, as if he ranked higher or had more time with the department.

Then there were the three people I'd never seen before. Two men and a woman. Their presence could be explained by the van with the logo from a neighboring city's police department.

Two of them were detectives, most likely, since they weren't uniformed officers. The third wore a lab coat and squatted near the ground, looking closely at something in the dirt inside the fenced pig pen, which was currently devoid of any swine occupants.

The three strangers must comprise an investigative unit, if I had to guess, brought in to process the crime scene.

Did that mean this was a crime scene? That those bones were human?

I swallowed and felt the tightness in my throat. I tried to overcome my panic and think about this logically.

Of course, this podunk town would call in a team from a bigger city for something like this. Just from being around Carson and that old ladies' group I knew what was considered big crime around here involved missing food.

Thoughts of Carson brought to the forefront of my

mind how odd it was that he wasn't here at the scene. What could that mean?

Was he off investigating Petunia's disappearance? Maybe he was off speaking with the poor old woman's family. I still couldn't figure out which one she was, but no doubt that was where Carson was.

If he'd been here, he be a distraction—and that could be either good or bad. Since the thoughts of these bones being tied to Declan had me passing out, I could use a distraction. But on the other hand, I needed to concentrate. Watch and listen. I didn't want to miss a thing in case there was some clue about Declan.

I decided it was for the best that he was absent. If Carson were here, I know my eyes, and my mind, would stray to him.

There was no getting around it. I wasn't the kind of girl who could have sex with no strings. At the moment, I really wished I were. With this situation possibly coming to a head, my imminent departure grew nearer with every day.

Emotional attachments were the last thing I needed. Unfortunately, second only to wanting to find my brother, being with Carson was what I most wanted.

All thoughts of my ill-timed love life fled when one of the Morgan brothers, the oldest, headed directly toward me.

He stopped just at the edge of the cornfield.

I froze, not wanting to move and give away my presence. I knew from my trek through the field exactly how much noise the innocuous looking stalks could make when I brushed against them.

I tried to breathe as softly as I could, afraid that even that would tip off the guy standing just feet from me.

Shit. Had I been spotted?

No.

He was digging in his pocket for his cell phone. He hit to answer a call and pressed the phone to his ear. He'd left the others to take the call. He hadn't seen me.

Phew.

"Harper, I kind of have my hands full here—"

"Petunia was kidnapped and they're going to kill her!" Stone had been cut off by the woman I could hear through the cell even though it wasn't on speakerphone.

"Wait. What?" he asked.

"Petunia's missing. Didn't you get my message?"

"No, I guess I missed it. We're a little busy here—"

"The Warriors took her. They posted about it on Facebook. They hinted they're going to butcher her."

Were the Warriors a local gang? Did Mudville have gangs?

And why would they want to kill Petunia? Maybe she wasn't an old lady after all, but rather involved with something shady. The local drug trade maybe.

What the hell kind of town was this that it could so

effectively hide its seedy underbelly beneath small town quirky charm?

Even I, who'd been looking pretty deeply, hadn't seen any indication of Mudville's dark side.

Stone—at least I think that was his name—started pacing in front of my little patch of corn camouflage, bringing my attention back to him and how precariously close we were.

"Wait. Harper. Calm down. How do you know all this?"

"I told you. Facebook!"

He let out a huff. "I don't think that Facebook is a very reliable source."

"It doesn't matter. We can't take a chance. We're on the way over there now."

"Over where? And who is *we*?" he asked.

"Agnes, Carson, me, Alice Mudd and Mary Brimley. We're going to Walton to confront the guy in charge of the Warriors and make him call in all of his members and demand to know where they have Petunia."

Stone swore softly. "Carson's with you?"

My ears perked up when I heard Carson's name.

"Yes."

He blew out a breath. "Thank God for that, at least."

"We were going with or without him," Harper announced.

"I'm sure you were." He snorted. "Please be careful. Okay?"

"Don't worry. Agnes has her shotgun."

"Um, what?" Stone's pacing came to a dead stop.

"Aunt Agnes. She brought that old double barrel she keeps in her bedroom."

"Jesus." Stone pulled the phone away from his head and delivered a few more choice obscenities for me and the corn stalks to hear before he pressed the cell back to his ear. "Carson is okay with Agnes bringing a gun?"

"Well, he didn't arrest her, so yeah. I guess so."

I was having trouble believing my ears. Apparently, that Agnes was one bad ass bitch. I'd have to reconsider my opinion of this ladies' society.

Could those old women be the Mudville version of the mob back in Boston?

Were they keeping the local rival gangs in check? Maintaining peace with their guns in between gossip and gab fests.

Knitting and knee breaking. It would be funny in any other situation.

I should be watching and listening to the bone investigation. But Stone's conversation had distracted me—understandably so. Maybe I needed to learn more about these Warriors.

For the first time since arriving, I wished Connor were here with me. Or my uncle or father.

I'd even settle for my grandmother. She'd lived the

life of a mob wife. Suffered the loss for it. She'd fit right in with Mudville's lady bosses. Hell, she could lead them.

But without any backup, I was starting to feel out of my depths. I might have grown up around that dark, dangerous world, but I'd done my best to stay on the periphery and uninvolved in it.

Technically, I had.

I never dated anyone connected—one reason why my number of boyfriends was so low. In my town it was hard to find someone not involved with the mob. I'd gotten out as soon as I'd graduated and gone away to school. Not far—still in state—but far enough.

The familial connection would forever be a part of me. I'd be tethered to that world by my blood alone. For life. But as for the day-to-day? Nope.

My nose was clean. Too clean. Right now, with bones, kidnappings, gangs and guns entering the picture, I could use some first-hand experience with playing dirty. Something other than what I'd heard when I'd been eavesdropping on the men in my family while growing up.

A flurry of activity by the pig pen had both Stone and me perking up. I peered between the corn and past him to where it looked like they were getting ready to remove the bones from their muddy grave.

I swallowed away the nausea as evidence bags were brought out and loaded with the possibly human remains.

One piece at a time.

I would have assumed it would be easier—less real—to see the individual bones rather than a whole skeleton.

It wasn't.

The fact that could be my brother—literally torn to pieces—had me holding down the vomit.

Thank goodness the action spurred Stone into ending the strange phone call with Harper. He basically brushed her off, pocketed the cell and trotted back to the group.

"What's happening?" he asked.

"They have to run more tests but their initial opinion is they're human," Stone's one brother, I think Cash was his name, said.

The youngest-looking brother, Boone, nodded. "Yup."

"Jesus." Stone shook his head. "Any idea who?"

"None," the sheriff answered. "Nothing was with the body. No wallet or clothes. But…"

There was a *but*. I drew in a breath and held it.

"There are teeth," the sheriff continued.

"You can identify the person by dental records," Stone guessed.

"Yup. That's the hope."

"And until then?" an older man, who looked too much like the boys to be anyone other than their father, asked.

"Until then, I guess you can put your pigs back in

the pen," the one investigator said.

"You sure?" Stone asked. "Should we maybe dig around a bit with the backhoe and make sure there aren't more?"

"Jeez. You want more bones?" Cash asked. "What? These weren't enough for you?"

"I just thought…" Stone let the sentence trail off.

"Where there's some, there could be more?" The youngest brother nodded. "Yup. That's what I'm thinking."

The woman, who I guessed was Stone's mother, covered her mouth with her hand, apparently as sickened by this conversation as I was.

The father shook his head. "Put the pigs back in the pen. One body's enough for me in one day." He turned on a boot heel and headed toward the house.

After a second, the woman nodded then turned to scurry after her husband.

"So what do we do?" Cash asked.

"You heard him. We put the pigs back," Stone said.

The sound of a door slamming had me jumping as my gaze shot to the parked vehicles.

"We're heading out," the woman told the group.

"You'll keep me updated?" the sheriff asked.

The detective nodded. "Will do."

Then they loaded into their various vehicles and drove away. Possibly with what remained of my brother.

All I wanted to do was look for myself at the place where the bones had been found.

My thoughts were that maybe they'd missed something. Something I would notice that they didn't. What, I didn't know. But I had to do something.

Squatting in the corn field and waiting for the coast to be clear was killing me.

Twenty-minutes later, I was still there. What was taking them so long to put some pigs away?

Even when that was done, the Morgans hung around, doing other things.

What I knew about farming would fit on a cocktail napkin. But there seemed to be a lot of carrying of stuff. Buckets. Hoses. Hay. Food. Water.

And also a lot of animals being moved from one place to another. The pigs, of course. But also the horses were brought from the field to the barn.

Then, the unthinkable happened. The brothers all grabbed an empty bushel basket and walked directly at me.

Why?

I panicked. Then it hit me. They were coming to pick the corn.

Right where I was sitting.

I had to get out of there and fast or be discovered sitting in the corn field with no good excuse why.

As they came forward, I scrambled backward, crab walking on heels and hands. Backing up until I'd be far enough away and out of sight so I could stand and run. Get to my car and get away from here.

"What's that?" Boone asked.

"What was what?" Cash paused to look at his brother.

"I saw it too. Something's in the corn," Stone said, as I heard his footsteps crunching closer.

"Is it the dog?" Boone asked.

"Nah. Romeo is sound asleep on Bart's bed," Cash answered.

My only hope was that they'd keep talking about the dog and I could get away. But I'd been so busy looking forward, I hadn't been looking behind.

I heard a crash of corn stalks and then was up and on my feet, hauled there by two big hands grabbing me by the arms.

"What do we have here?" Stone said, turning me around to face him.

Boone crashed through the stalks to come stand next to his brother. "Hey. Isn't she the new bartender from the Long River Inn?"

"Yup." Cash, following right behind Boone, nodded before asking me, "What the hell are you doing in here?"

Then, things went from bad to worse as Carson appeared behind the brothers.

The shock was evident on his features as he said, "That's what I'd like to know."

21

CARSON

"Kayleigh, you need to tell me what's going on."

"Nothing. I was just curious about the bones." Sitting on the edge of her bed, she looked at me with those guileless eyes.

Oh, she was good. I almost believed her.

I'd brought her back to her apartment for this little chat, because I sure as hell didn't want to have it in front of the Morgans at the farm, or the sheriff at the station.

It was bad enough she'd had me going for weeks now, believing everything she said. I didn't need the embarrassment of anyone else knowing what a dupe I'd been.

Not anymore.

"The same bones that had you passing out when you first heard about them?" I asked, doubtful.

"I told you. I forgot to eat. That's why I was lightheaded."

She was lying. I didn't want to admit it and I hated that I knew it to be true. But it was.

"Lightheaded is a mild way of putting falling flat on the floor. And you were supposed to be resting. That's why Laney covered the bar. To give you time to recuperate. Not so you could go sneaking around the Morgan's cornfield."

"I felt better." She shrugged, which only made me angry.

"If you'd felt better, you would have gone back to work." I sighed.

Why was I even arguing with her? I wasn't going to get a straight answer.

She'd probably been lying to me all along. About all sorts of things.

Why? Who was she really? I should probably do some legwork and find out because I was starting to think I was sleeping with the enemy.

Thinking back, there had been odd things all along.

I still had no idea why she had been parked in front of Buck's house the other night. Or why I found her parked in front of the library that night of the first meeting. But it was pretty clear it wasn't that she dozed off after getting food at the diner.

Shaking my head, I was having trouble even looking at the woman. What made it feel like a knife stuck in my gut was that I had started to fall for her. Hard.

I'd actually been eying my house this morning as I got ready for work, picturing where Kayleigh and her things would fit in if I asked her to move in with me some time down the road.

Stupid.

It was obvious I didn't know her at all. And the more I thought about it, the madder I got. At myself. At her.

"Kayleigh—" I cut myself off rather than cuss at her.

I was, after all, in uniform. I had to be a deputy now and not her incredibly gullible lover.

Jesus. I ran a hand over my face, trying to regain my composure.

I was mad enough to punch a wall until a new thought struck me.

Maybe she was in trouble and that's why she was lying. Was she on the run? Maybe from an abusive relationship or something else out of her control. She could be an innocent in all this.

God, how I hoped she was an innocent in all this.

I decided to try a different tact. I squatted down to be able to talk to her eye-to-eye where she sat.

"If you tell me what's really going on, maybe I can help."

Her eyes turned glassy as she shook her head.

Call me crazy, but they looked like real tears. Of

course, what the hell did I know? I was the one who'd believed every word that came out of her mouth until this afternoon.

"You can't tell me? Or you just don't want to?"

She opened her mouth and drew in a stuttering breath. "I can't."

"Why not?"

She continued to shake her head as the tears fell. But instead of garnering sympathy, all those big fat drops streaking down her cheeks did was make me angry again.

"I can't help you if you don't talk to me. I mean I know why I don't trust you anymore. But I've never given you a reason to not trust me." The words came out sharper than I'd intended.

I couldn't help it. I was watching the whole future I'd stupidly created in my mind crumble and fall.

"I'm sorry," she whispered.

"Are you really sorry? Or just sorry I don't blindly believe you anymore?" I shook my head, staring at the corner of the room to avoid looking at her.

I had no evidence she was doing anything illegal. All I knew was what my gut was telling me. What it had been telling me all along, but I'd ignored it.

Her excuses didn't make sense. She showed up at odd places, at odd times, and what hurt the most—the kick in the gut—was that she'd lied to me. Probably about everything.

I couldn't arrest her. I couldn't even bring her in

for questioning. Crawling around in the Morgan's cornfield might be trespassing, but the family hadn't pressed charges.

My wave of relief over that fact, that I wouldn't have to bring her in, increased my anger.

I was still protecting her. Still had feelings for her. Even now.

I had to get out of there before I lost my mind.

"I gotta go." I stood, about to turn, when she reached out and grabbed my arm.

"Carson, I *can't* tell you. It's not a choice. It's dangerous. It's life or death."

The raw emotion exposed by the intensity of her words stopped my exit. I grabbed both her hands and sat on the edge of the mattress next to her.

"I can protect you."

She let out a tear-filled breathy laugh. "No. You can't. And it's just not me. There are… others I have to protect."

Others. What others? Who was she protecting and why?

Jesus. Did she have a kid? Was she hiding from the baby's daddy?

Plots worthy of all those television crime shows I succumbed to on the many nights I was home alone ran through my head.

It didn't matter. No matter what it was, I could deal with it.

"Kayleigh, I've got the law on my side."

She shook her head. "Where I come from, we can't trust the law."

"The city? Why not?" I reviewed any news stories that had come out of New York City involving the police, searching for an answer.

A brief moment of panic showed in her eyes. As if she'd decided she'd said too much.

Lips pressed tightly, she just shook her head again. But beneath the stubbornness, beneath the fear, I could tell she wanted to trust me.

That was evident in how tightly she gripped my hands. Like I was a lifeline.

I extricated my hands from hers and pressed her face between my palms, bringing my face close to hers.

"If you can't talk to me as a deputy, then talk to me as a friend." My heart beat faster as I added, "As your boyfriend."

This close, her face was out of focus, but I could see the pain mingled with longing as she said, "Then you could end up dead too."

She was trying to protect me as well as this mystery person or people and herself?

As scared and desperate as she was, she was still worried about me. My chest tightened at the knowledge.

But protect me from what? What was going on?

That huge, looming question took a step back, replaced by all my many emotions about this girl.

Despite it all, I cared. The word *loved* flashed through my head, but I refused to let it linger.

More than that, I wanted her. The adrenaline. The anger. The frustration. It all morphed into an overwhelming need to take her. Possess her body if I couldn't have her trust or her truth.

Before I could think better of it, I pressed my lips against hers in a searing kiss filled with all the emotions I couldn't fight.

Her hands came up to cup my face as she kissed me back with a fervor that told me she was feeling the same way I was.

I shouldn't be kissing her. I didn't have any reason to trust her, but for some reason I did.

All the *should nots* and *don'ts* disappeared with that kiss.

There wasn't a moment of hesitation in either of us as we tumbled backward onto the mattress.

Frenzy had me tearing at the button at her waist while she yanked the bottom of my uniform shirt up and out from where it had been tucked in.

I felt the smooth warm skin of her belly against my palm as I shoved my hand down inside her underwear.

She gasped when I reached the heat of her core and set to work.

My fingers strummed her into a frenzied crescendo. Into a keening, writhing, glorious climax that had me jumping off the bed to ditch my clothes so I could join her in the pleasure.

I needed to feel her surrounding me. I covered myself quickly with the condom I'd luckily stuffed into the little slot in my wallet this morning. Back before all hell had broken loose in Mudville. Before there were kidnapped mascots and human bones in the pig pen.

None of that seemed to matter as I slid inside her.

When her gaze locked onto mine it felt like her walls dropped away. I could see the vulnerability. The fear. The emotions. And call me crazy, but it all looked genuine.

Now that I knew for a fact she'd been lying to me about other things, and I'd accepted that and believed it was for a good—if undisclosed—reason, I was a better judge of what was real and what wasn't when it came to Kayleigh.

I no longer suppressed my instincts. I embraced them. Listened to them. And my gut told me this—between us now—was all real.

Women have used sex to control and to deceive men for thousands of years. Cleopatra had Marc Antony wrapped around her little finger and I'd bet she'd done it with sex.

That wasn't the case here. I might have been clueless about the truth last night. But today I'd come to her bed with my eyes wide open.

I might regret that decision, but right now, as I bottomed out inside this woman, I had no regrets.

A whole world of pleasure opened up to me as her

body gripped my length while she cried out my name and came apart beneath me.

Then I knew, I'd do anything to save her. Anything.

Even if it cost me my career.

Or my life.

22

KAYLEIGH

I knew Carson wanted me to tell him everything. Just as I knew I couldn't.

His plea hung unspoken in the ear as we sat up, side-by-side in my bed and sipped the coffee I'd made us in the coffee maker that sat on top of the mini fridge.

He glanced around the room as the early morning sunlight streamed through the window and highlighted the dust dancing in the air. "This really isn't a bad little apartment. You've got all the necessities."

This new observation was just one of the many in a long run. Carson's attempt at making conversation while steering clear of the elephant in the room. The topic that shall not be named. The secret I wouldn't tell him.

I appreciated the effort, but I'd be lying if I didn't

admit avoiding the subject might be more awkward than just facing it. But since it was obvious this was how he wanted to play it, I'd play along.

I forced a smile. "Yup. All the comforts of a luxury hotel room. All this can be yours for just a hundred bucks a week. But you'd probably have to work at the bar too. That might get in the way of your real job—"

Uh, oh. I'd done it. I'd accidentally brought up the subject we'd been avoiding. The fact he worked for the sheriff's department and now knew I was hiding something. Something big. Something bad.

He pressed his lips together and nodded. After drawing in a deep breath, he said, "Speaking of my job—"

I braced myself for the conversation.

"I'd better get moving. I should go in early. Since I never got back into the office yesterday afternoon…"

He tipped his head to indicate the bed where we'd spent the late afternoon. And the night.

"I never got around to filing the report on Petunia." He swung his legs over the edge of the mattress and stood, gloriously naked.

I sat up straighter. Not from his nudity, though that was nice, but over the topic of Petunia.

Here was a conversation I was interested in. "What happened with that?"

He bent to pick up his underwear and pants from the floor. "Nothing. Petunia's back home, safe and sound. And there's now a group of boys on Walton

High's football team who won't be playing in the next five games because of what they did."

"They were high school boys?" I asked.

The Warriors recruited their gang members young. Although, I guess the Irish mob did too. I remembered Connor running messages back and forth for them from when he was about eleven.

"Yup." He nodded, pulling on his shirt. "Just a prank but it has to be punished. It caused a lot of people a lot of grief. Not to mention my time."

"Well, I'm glad Petunia is okay," I said, watching as he zipped up his uniform pants.

But if it wasn't Petunia's bones in that pig pen, the question that had me sick to my stomach remained. Whose were they?

Carson was dressed now. He'd be leaving and I still had hours before I had to be behind the bar. Now might be my one chance to grab the memory card from the game camera I'd set up by the library.

Otherwise, it would have to wait until tonight. But that might not work. If I were with Carson tonight, I wouldn't be able to sneak away to grab it.

Even with him knowing part of the story—a very small part—being with Carson was a hindrance to my search. But I couldn't bring myself to give him up.

So it had to be now.

He kissed me goodbye and left and that launched me into action. I showered, then shoved a stale dinner roll I'd grabbed at work a couple of days ago into my mouth while I got dressed.

The town would be bustling at this time of morning, but it couldn't be helped. I'd just have to grab the game camera quick and hope no one noticed.

If someone did see me and questioned why I was crawling around in the bushes by the library, I'd just claim I'd seen a stray kitten and was trying to grab it.

Cover story in place and ready, I grabbed my cell phone and my keys and headed out the door.

I was there in under five minutes. That was one good thing about this town. Something I'd miss when I left.

The thought of leaving gave me a stomachache. I was getting more and more attached to Carson. Leaving was going to suck.

I couldn't think of that now as the shadow of Declan possibly being buried in the pig pen hung over me. My love life had to be put on the back burner.

Parking as close to where I needed to be as I could, I looked right and left before sprinting from the car to the bushes that bordered the library building.

Ducking down, I grabbed the camera from one of the lower branches and ran back to my car.

Either I was really out of shape or the fear of checking the memory card had taken my breath away. I was breathing fast and hard, my hand shaking, as I pulled out the very thin memory card with just my fingernails.

I sat with it in my hand, looking around.

Shit. How was I going to check it? The inexpensive game cam didn't have a viewscreen.

I glanced down at my cell phone. I spun the device around, looking for a memory card slot. Nothing. Damn.

Wait. My tablet back in my room. That had a slot for a memory card so people could add extra storage. I needed to get home.

I threw the car into gear. Checking the road, I pulled out onto Main Street and spun around in a messy and possibly illegal U-turn. Then I was speeding toward the bar, breaking the speed limit by a good twenty miles per hour. I was sleeping with the local deputy so I was pretty sure even if I got pulled over, Carson would get me out of it.

Sex with Carson had benefits—besides the obvious amazing physical ones.

But even with as good as being with Carson had been, everything except the memory card in my cupholder flew out of my brain.

The moment I got to my room, I grabbed my tablet —and realized it was dead.

Delivering a few choice words over that, I tore around the room looking for the charger. Finally, I found it and plugged it into the wall.

It seemed to take forever for the tablet to power on. Sitting on the floor next to the outlet with the tablet in my lap, I noticed my hands shaking as I tried to put the card into the slot.

Once it was in, I had to figure out where to look on the device to locate the files. Eventually, I found the right place.

I opened the first of many pictures. So many, I was surprised the card hadn't run out of storage. Good thing I hadn't been cheap. I'd gotten the highest capacity one the store had.

In the past week since I'd installed it but never got around to checking the memory card, it had stored a lot of pictures. Thousands.

It was set to only record motion but there was a lot of motion at the library.

After reviewing the first few hundred photos my eyes were glazing over.

I saw more people come and go than I knew lived in this tiny town. I did learn that Alice was surprisingly well-read. She visited the library nearly every day that week, coming and going with a stack of hardcover books most times.

Besides that moderately entertaining tidbit, checking the photos was mind-numbing work.

I started to pay less attention to the daytime ones, barely scanning those, and more attention to the ones taken at night. That was when I assumed Declan would be coming and going—if he was there at all. That was still questionable.

While speeding through, one picture caught my eye. But I had been on a roll, scrolling through so fast

I passed it. I had to stop and back up to get to it again.

What I saw stole my breath.

I'd know my brother anywhere. Even in a grainy black and white photo taken in night vision mode by the camera.

He was here.

He was alive.

But wait. When was this photo taken? Was this picture from before the bones were discovered? Or after?

I scanned the picture and noticed the small numbers in the corner. The date and time. That was exactly what I needed. But the date was all wrong. It showed January from the year two-thousand.

Crap. I must have had to set the correct date on the camera to make it work. I hadn't.

How could I be so careless? The date was critical information. Information I needed. If he'd been at the library after the bones were discovered, it would confirm Declan was alive.

But now I had proof. He was here in Mudville. It had been all I'd wished for. Proof.

But now that I had it, I wasn't sure I wanted it. Because since Declan was here, those bones very well could be his.

CARSON

It wasn't something I wanted to do. It was something I had to do. That didn't make it any easier to swallow for me.

I sat at my desk, fingers poised on the keyboard on my computer and typed in Kayleigh's license plate number.

When the results populated my screen, I leaned forward. The car was registered to Kayleigh Walsh of Charlestown, Massachusetts.

She'd said she was from the city. Although now I couldn't remember if she'd actually said New York City or if I'd just assumed that.

Again, a lie that was not quite a lie. Shadows of deception but not a blatant, outright fallacy. I leaned back and considered how good she was at doing that and what I was going to do about her. About this whole damn situation.

I needed more facts. More information. And though it felt wrong on so many levels to do it, I needed to do a deep dive into Kayleigh. Starting with checking if the woman I'd spent the night with—the woman I'd fallen for—had a criminal record.

"You're here early." The sheriff's arrival, when I'd been concentrating so hard on my computer screen, startled me.

I leaned back and tried to look casual and not like I'd just been investigating my girlfriend, the possible criminal. "Yeah, well, with all the excitement yesterday, there's a lot of paperwork to do today."

The sheriff snorted. "You got that right. Any word from the forensics team on the bones?"

"John didn't say anything before he left and I didn't see any messages."

"Shit. This feels like we're sitting on a powder keg waiting to see if it goes off."

I knew exactly how he felt only instead of a pile of bones, my powder keg was soft and curvy and felt far too good beneath me.

Nodding, I made some noncommittal grunt of agreement.

"What happened with Petunia?" he asked.

Another delicate subject. I'd have to dance around the truth on this one too. It struck me maybe Kayleigh and I weren't that different. I was about to be vague and deliver to the sheriff a load of half-truths myself.

I couldn't tell him I'd accompanied a posse of

women, one of whom was armed with a loaded antique double-barrel shotgun, on a hunt for the kids who'd taken the pig. So, I kept it simple.

"I have to give credit to Harper on that one. She found a post on social media. The Walton football team was hinting that they had Petunia. I met up with the team's coach. He did most of the work. Called in the team. They returned the pig to Agnes. And he's handling the punishments with the school. I figured that was all right since it's technically not our jurisdiction anyway."

The sheriff nodded. "Agreed. Let Walton deal with their own hooligans. We've got enough troubles of our own here."

Wasn't that the truth.

The older man moved to the coffee maker, where there was no coffee since I'd been so busy investigating Kayleigh, I'd never gotten around to making a pot this morning.

"No coffee?" he asked.

"Uh, sorry. I got distracted. I'll make a pot now."

"I can do it. I was making coffee probably before you were born."

Judging by the looks of the department's coffee maker, he might have been doing it on that exact machine. There was a reason why I usually swung by the bakery to grab a cup on my way in along with a honey bun.

I hadn't even done that today. This thing with Kayleigh had me so torn up I didn't have an appetite.

There was only one way out of this. I needed to find out as much as possible, if only to prove to myself, and everyone else if needed, that she was innocent.

With the sheriff occupied with making his coffee, I turned back to the computer.

Braced for what I'd find, I didn't breathe freely again until she came up clean.

No criminal record.

That was a very good sign. But it also meant I had to dig deeper to find what I was looking for. Who she was afraid of. Who she was protecting. And why.

I needed to check out her known associations and family. I started hitting keys, pawing deeper into her life.

It felt like snooping. I had to remind myself this was my job. Crimes had been committed here in Mudville. I still didn't think she was a suspect in those, but she definitely knew something. More than what she was saying.

Since she wasn't talking, I had to dig. And what I unearthed had my mouth dropping open.

After a quick glance to make sure the sheriff wasn't nearby, I leaned closer to the screen, trying to wrap my head around what I read.

Kayleigh's family had mob ties.

Her uncle had close associations to one of the big

Irish crime families in Boston. He'd done some hard time for his crimes.

Her father had managed to stay out of jail, but I'd bet he was just as deep in it as his brother.

Then there was her grandfather. After years of being suspected of multiple crimes—including homicide—but never convicted for them, he'd turned up dead thirteen years ago. Found floating in the Charles River with two bullets in his head.

Jesus.

Was this it? Was she running from the mob?

She'd said she was trying to protect someone else. Her family maybe? After she'd lived through what had happened to her grandfather, her fear, her secrecy, her lack of trust would all make sense.

At least now I knew what I was up against. That didn't mean I knew what to do about it.

I could start tailing her maybe. See what she was up to.

It might be the only way to help her, even if she didn't want my help.

My cell phone buzzed with a calendar reminder. I glanced down at the readout and narrowed my eyes at the message.

Meeting Tonight Library Committee 6PM

My initial dread and annoyance was quickly replace when a plan formed. The meeting was the perfect excuse. I could tell Kayleigh I couldn't see her tonight.

She'd think, with me busy with the meeting for hours, the coast was clear. Only instead, I was going to beg out of the meeting and wait to tail her after she got off work.

With any luck she'd let her guard down and lead me straight to something I'd find useful. Something that would provide answers. Because right now, all I had were more questions.

24

KAYLEIGH

Carson had said he'd be at the library meeting from six until probably nine tonight. As much as I felt for him for having to endure a three-hour meeting with the biddies, the timing couldn't have been more fortunate.

I'd told him I was going to go to bed early and I'd see him tomorrow.

As I sat in my parked car and waited for the last remnants of daylight from the setting sun to disappear, I only felt a little bit guilty over that lie.

I glanced at the time.

Any minute now that stupid meeting would be over. Then I'd leave my car parked way down the block so Carson and Mary wouldn't spot it, and I'd sneak down to the library and wait for Declan.

The plan was all set. It might actually work too. If

it did, I could be with my brother in just hours. My heart raced at the thought.

The vibrating of my cell had me frowning at the interruption. When I saw Laney's name on the display, that frown deepened.

"Hey. What's up?" I asked.

"I hate to ask this, but can you cover the bar? Carter cut his hand pretty badly slicing lemons. I can't cover the kitchen and the bar at the same time. No one else I called to come in is picking up their phones."

"Um. Yeah. Sure. I'll be there in two minutes."

"Great. Thank you." She hung up, cutting off the loud background noises of the bar.

Shit. With one wistful glance down the block, I started my engine and spun the car around toward work.

I'd just gotten behind the bar when the front door opened and Carson walked in.

"Hey."

"Hey."

"Meeting over already?"

"Yeah. Uh, earlier than expected tonight. What are you doing here?"

"Carter cut his hand slicing fruit. Laney just called and checked on him. He's at the ER getting stitches."

Carson shook his head. "Man. He's going to hate that, because you know I'm going to have to tease him for being careless with a deadly fruit knife."

I smiled. "The boy scout has an evil streak."

"Me? Nah." He grinned. "So, how long are you here for? Until closing?"

"I don't know. Until Laney says I can go. I guess once the kitchen officially closes, she can come out and take over the bar. I'm not sure."

"I was thinking maybe we could hang out when you get out of here." He looked at me not with the eyes of a man who wanted sex, but with the intense look of a man with questions.

That scared me. He was a man who wanted answers. And I was not a woman willing or able to give them.

"Tomorrow maybe? I'm so tired. I really just want to crash and sleep. I only came in because Laney was desperate."

"Understood. I guess neither of us got a full night's sleep last night." He smiled, but it didn't quite reach his eyes. "So, I guess I'll say goodnight and see you tomorrow."

"I look forward to it." I smiled.

He paused just a second, nodded one more time, then spun and headed for the door.

One bullet dodged. Now to get out of here…

I headed through the swinging door. "Kitchen closes at ten, right?" I asked.

"Yup." Laney nodded as she dumped raw potato wedges into the fryer. "You can head out after that. I know you already worked a full shift today."

"Thanks." I turned back toward the bar. My plan was back on. Just with a slight delay.

The hour and a half flew by. I kept busy cleaning up the mess Carter had left, closing out the tabs of a couple of customers and restocking supplies for the morning so I wouldn't have to do it tomorrow.

Before I knew it, Laney was beside me, telling me to take my tips and head out.

Gladly.

I grabbed the singles from the jar, shoved them in my pocket and headed out, not upstairs to my apartment, but to my car.

Back on Main Street I was too hyped up to sit around and wait. I decided that parking in hopes of spotting Declan hadn't worked so far. Maybe I needed to take a more active, hands-on approach.

I left the car down the block.

Keeping to the shadows, well out of the light from the streetlamps, I made my way to the side of the library.

I had to think like Declan. The smart thing to do would be hide out of sight during the day. Then sneak out at night to get provisions. So, how was he getting in and out?

The front door was unlocked that one time, but I'd bet old Roger and his minions made sure it was locked since then.

The windows maybe?

I looked up at the first floor sills far above my head.

Too high. But the basement… Those windows were ground level. I hit the button on my cell phone and used it as a flashlight.

The first window I checked had bars on it. I walked to the next one, the one farther from the road. It looked like the stone had crumbled enough that the bars had fallen out.

My heart sped as I bent lower and gave the window sash a push. It swung in easily from the hinge on the top.

I looked around me. No one was on the street. Or in the library building as far as I could tell. The windows upstairs were dark. There were no cars in the lot.

Everything seemed quiet. Deserted.

I eyed the window again. It was big enough for me to slip inside. But how far was the drop to the floor? The last thing I needed was to be trapped in the basement of the library with a broken leg.

Kneeling, I felt the cold damp dirt through my pants as I stuck my head and the flashlight inside. There were a couple of boxes right beneath the window. It looked like the basement was used for storage.

Those boxes would make the perfect steps for me to get inside without breaking my legs. More importantly, I'd be able to get out again after I'd looked around for any evidence Declan had been staying there.

On my hands and knees, I backed toward the window and I maneuvered my feet and then legs through. Then, using muscles I probably hadn't used since high school gym class, I braced my arms on the sill and tried to slowly lower myself down inside.

It was scary. I was going in basically blind, unable to see the boxes below me. Not being able to judge how far down they were I stretched my legs straight down, toes pointed, and searched for the box.

Just when my arms, shaking from the effort, were about to give out, I felt my toe hit something solid.

Relieved I dropped down and landed with both feet safely on the box.

The cardboard supported my weight and didn't collapse, which had been another concern. But this being a library, there was a good chance these boxes were filled with books, making them extra sturdy. Lucky for me.

Brushing the dirt from my hands, I turned toward the basement. I couldn't see anything in the dark so I reached again for the cell phone in my back pocket. I was trying to navigate to the flashlight app to light my way for my search when hands came out of the dark.

I screamed as they grabbed me with an iron grasp on both of my arms. The person threw me hard across the room with enough force it knocked me to the ground.

My cell phone flew out of my hand. It landed facedown, its beam pointing upward like a beacon illuminating the stone foundation and the window through which I'd crawled.

From my position on the dirty hard floor, I could see the shadowy figure use the box as a step to vault up to the window opening.

This person didn't want to hurt me. He wanted to escape. And when the beam of light hit on his face I knew why.

"Declan? Stop! It's me." My voice stopped him.

Braced in the window's opening, he swiveled his head to look straight at me. I lunged for my cell and held it so he could see my face.

"Kayleigh? Jaysus. What are you doing here?"

Hearing my brother's voice again was overwhelming. Tears of relief clouded my eyes. "I'm looking for you."

Declan stepped down and offered me a hand. He pulled me up from the floor and into a hug.

"How the feck did you track me here?" he asked.

Declan, born here just like me, didn't have the soft brogue from childhood years spent in Ireland like Connor. But he had picked up Connor's—and our parents'—distinctly Irish cuss words.

Much like his Boston accent, the Irish words really got more prevalent when he was emotional.

"I used the *Find my Phone* app. Remember? You took my old cell when I upgraded to the new one. It was still on there and active."

"Fuck me. I knew I should have ditched that phone earlier."

"Why in the world, of all the places you could have gone, did you choose to come here?" I asked.

"Not a choice really." He shrugged. "It's just where I landed."

A short laugh escaped me. "Come on. No one just lands in Mudville."

"I lifted a motorcycle in Boston and drove until the gas ran out. Then I walked for a bit along the highway. Got a ride with a long hauler I met at a truck stop. He stopped here in town at the diner. I decided it was a good place to hide. I mean seriously. Who would look for me here?"

Why?" I asked. "Why are you running?"

He tipped his head to one side. "You know why."

"No, I really don't." I let out a breath. "Declan, I thought we'd agreed you'd stay out of it. Both of us would. It was too late for dad and gramps and Uncle Jimmy. Even Connor was too involved, just being an errand boy. But you. Declan, you were clear of it all."

He shook his head. "I screwed up, Kay."

"But why?"

"Money. I figured I could do just one bank job. Drive the getaway car in exchange for ten percent of the take. It was a two-million-dollar job, minimum. You know what we could do with that kind of cash? I was going to settle up Ma and Pa's mortgage on our house. Pay off your student loan."

Teary-eyed, I shook my head. "No. Please do not tell me you did this for me."

I couldn't live with the guilt.

"Not just for you. I was gonna buy me a wicked sweet ride with some of that money too."

All I could do was continue to shake my head in disbelief.

He'd ruined his life. All our lives. For money.

"I didn't think it would be a big deal. One and done. Then no more. I'd be out," he continued.

"It doesn't work that way with those people. It never has. You know that."

"I negotiated it before the job," Declan explained.

"You trusted them to live up to their end of the bargain?" My voice rose to a dangerous level. If someone were walking by outside, they could hear me. I drew in a breath and started again, softer, "Don't you know once you're in, you can never get out? At least, not alive."

"I thought since they'd agreed up front..." He shrugged.

"So what happened?" Obviously, his plan hadn't worked out so well.

"We did the job. I went to get my cut after. They said they'd give it to me *if* I agreed to work another bank job the following week. I told them no. I wanted out. Like we agreed."

"What did they do?"

"They said we had a new agreement now. I keep

working for them until they said I didn't have to any longer. Then they, uh, roughed me up a little."

I gasped.

"I'm fine. Nothing I couldn't handle. But they told me to go home and think about where my loyalties were. Then they told me to say hello to Grams for them."

My chest tightened at that veiled threat from the men who'd most likely killed my grandfather.

"So you ran. And you've been sleeping here in the basement since?" I glanced around the dim space.

He nodded. "Yeah."

"Come stay with me. No one will see you. I have my own apartment. No one comes there."

No one except Carson, who would be the worst person to find Declan. But that could be avoided. I'd just suggest we start hanging out at Carson's place instead of mine.

Mine was so small. I didn't even have a table and chairs or television or stove. I didn't think he'd question my request.

"I don't know, Kay…" Declan hesitated.

"No. Declan, I won't take no for an answer. I'm not leaving you here."

I could tell he was tempted. Who wouldn't be?

It was damp and smelly down here. Not to mention the spiderwebs. Just the sight of them everywhere had me feeling like things were crawling on me.

And I strongly suspected he was using that bucket in the corner as a toilet, judging by the roll of toilet paper next to it.

"Come on, Declan. Come with me."

Finally, he nodded. "All right. But just for tonight."

"Just for tonight," I agreed…for now.

I led the way to the window. He offered me his hand to steady me as I climbed up on top of the box.

Before I attempted to crawl out the high window, a thought hit me.

I turned back to him. "Declan, you didn't happen to kill someone and feed them to the pigs at the farm down the road, did you?"

He drew back. "What? No. Why would you ask that?"

Phew. I shook my head. "No reason."

I turned back to grip the windowsill while he grabbed me around the waist and boosted me up. I was leaving that basement with more hope than I'd had going in. More than I'd had in weeks.

Things were definitely looking up.

25

CARSON

Consciousness arrived slowly. I went from dreams of kissing Kayleigh to startling awake, alone in my car with a hard-on.

Shit. I'd fallen asleep. I was supposed to be watching for her to leave after her shift. To see if she'd sneak out.

Glancing at the clock I saw it was close to sunrise. I'd slept almost the whole damn night here hidden in the corner of the parking lot.

I squinted through the darkness to the portion of the parking lot illuminated by the streetlamp. Her car was parked there. If Kayleigh had snuck out last night, she was back now.

What did it say about me that I couldn't even stay awake for a simple stake out? Even after the two to-go cups of coffee in the console next to me. Hell of a deputy I was.

I stretched and it seemed like I could feel every bone and muscle in my body.

My legs were cramped. My back was stiff. My butt was numb. And I had to piss.

I definitely wasn't cut out for this shit. I was glad Mudville policing rarely involved all night stake outs.

Luckily the sun wasn't up yet. I still had the cover of darkness as I reached for the key in the ignition.

I'd parked my SUV way off in the back of the parking lot, half hidden by bushes, so no one should have seen me.

It wouldn't do for one of Mudville's deputies to be spotted sleeping one off in the parking lot of the local bar.

Even if that weren't the case, it's what they'd assume. And what they'd gossip about today and for weeks to come.

With one final glance at Kayleigh's car, parked innocently in the spot at the bottom of the stairs that led to her apartment, just where it had been yesterday, I headed for home.

There wasn't enough time to sleep more. So I showered, changed clothes and grabbed a cup of coffee. Then I headed to work, early again today.

It couldn't hurt having the sheriff see me be extra diligent and getting to work early. Especially since half of my time and attention was being spent worrying about Kayleigh rather than working.

Not to mention that my usual half-hour lunch had

stretched to be over an hour lately since I'd been going out to the bar to eat rather than grabbing a sandwich and eating at my desk like I used to.

But after I walked in this morning and saw the massive stacks of paper on John Callahan's desk I had to wonder if I'd be going anywhere for lunch today.

"What's all this?" I asked him.

He looked up, bleary-eyed.

"Thank God, you're here." He stood and gathered one tall pile, carrying it over to my desk where he dropped it with a thud. "Tag. You're it."

I frowned at the pile still wondering what it was.

"The sheriff decided we need to update. So we have to scan every paper report in the file room, save it to the cloud then box up the papers and put them in storage."

The man who still had a rotary phone wanted to go digital? And use the cloud?

"That's gonna be a lot of paperwork to scan," I observed.

"You're telling me. I only got two years' worth done and I've been working on it all night. I was just about to start on the next year. Take my advice. Tackle it one year at a time."

I sighed. "All right. I'll get on it."

John slapped a yellow sticky note to the top of the pile. "This is how he wants us to name the files."

I frowned down at the complicated format. "What the hell brought this on?"

"He had a sheriff's association dinner last night. Apparently, they had a speaker who thinks digital records is the shit. He came directly here after the dinner, a few beers in him, and told me to start scanning."

"Wow." Maybe we needed to get him to quit that organization if it was going to produce this much work for us.

"Have fun," John said, looking too happy to be passing on this job to me.

"Yeah. Thanks."

John couldn't get out of here fast enough. He was gone in under sixty seconds, disappearing with a cloud of dust in the parking lot.

As the door had swung shut behind him, I reached for my cell. Before I got buried in paperwork, I wanted to shoot off a text to Kayleigh. Tell her I wouldn't be able to get away for lunch and ask if she wanted to get together after work.

I felt guilty the moment I hit send. It was early. I'd forgotten how early.

She might be sleeping. Although, from the time we'd spent together, I'd seen she kept her cell on vibrate. So maybe my text wouldn't wake her. She could read it when she woke.

To my surprise, Kayleigh texted right back.

I picked it up and tapped the screen to call her back. She answered with a soft, "Hello."

"Hi. You're up. I thought you might sleep late after working an extra shift last night."

"Nah. That would have been nice but, uh, you know me. Sleep isn't my best skill so... anyway. I'd love to hang out tonight. But could we do it at your place?"

She was still speaking so softly I could barely hear her. It made her sound extra sexy so I didn't ask her to speak up. Instead, I pressed the side buttons to raise the volume on my cell.

"My place? Yeah. Sure."

I racked my brain to remember the last time I'd washed my sheets. Whenever it was, it wasn't in the last week.

Shit. I'd have to go home after work and do laundry, because with any luck, Kayleigh and I would be in my bed tonight.

But I could worry about all that housekeeping stuff later. For now, I wanted to catch up with what was happening in Kayleigh's secretive world.

"So, anything new with you?" I asked.

"Since I saw you last night at the bar?" She laughed. It was a light, casual sound. "Nope. Not a whole lot of excitement happens on the commute between the bar and my apartment. I went right to bed."

I listened closely and evaluated if she was being *too* casual before saying, "Yeah, I guess not. So, why do you suddenly want to come hang out at my house?"

"We've been, you know, *seeing* each other a lot

lately and I realized I don't even know where you live," she explained.

Seeing each other was one way to describe what we did at night together.

"That's true," I agreed.

"And I'm thinking your place has *got* to be nicer than my apartment so..."

"I don't know. I'm kind of fond of your apartment. Lots of good memories there," I said, perfectly truthfully. "But you're right. My place is bigger. And you're also right that after all the time we've been spending together, you probably should see where I live. So, yes. I'd love to have you over tonight."

"Great. You'll have to text me the address."

"Or I can come pick you up."

"Um, okay. I guess. What time?"

"Six-thirty?" That would give her time to get off work, and me time to get home, change and straighten up.

"Okay. I'll be ready and waiting for you downstairs," she said.

"I can come upstairs—"

"Nope. It's fine. I'll be outside waiting for you."

"Uh. All right. See you then."

"See you." Then she was gone.

When the call went dead, I lowered the cell from my ear and considered the conversation.

There wasn't really anything suspicious about

Kayleigh wanting to come over. Or meeting me outside to get picked up.

So why was my intuition setting off alarms?

In my head and in my gut.

Pretty much every fiber of my being was screaming something wasn't right here. Yet, I couldn't pinpoint exactly what was off. All I knew was that something was.

I only hoped I could figure it out before it was too late.

26

KAYLEIGH

Deputy Carson Bekker lived in a beautiful little cottage set back from the road on one of the tree-lined, dead-end side streets in Mudville.

Close enough to town to be convenient. Far enough away it didn't have that living-in-a-fishbowl feel to it that the houses on Main Street must have.

The house had white shingles and black shutters and a front door painted in a sunny, welcoming, bright yellow.

The overflowing flower beds that flanked the front door were an explosion of color and made me feel like I had stepped into a fairytale. Add a white picket fence and this would have been the home out of my childhood dreams.

The kind of house I imagined my Barbie doll living in with Ken. Or me living in one day when—if—I ever left Charlestown and found my dream man.

And it was the dead last place I'd pictured when I'd imagined where Carson lived.

I thought my excuse for coming here tonight instead of hanging out at my place had been a bullshit lie to protect Declan. It hadn't turned out to be such bullshit after all.

Now that I was here, in his home, it didn't seem like a lie anymore. This house was like a window into his life. Seeing where he lived had opened up a whole new side of him to me.

The space was neat and clean, but not obsessively so. It was definitely a place that was lived in.

Comfortable. A bit shabby even, in a charming way, with its faded upholstery on the big over-stuffed chair in front of the window and the worn spots on the arms of the sofa.

I liked it. A lot.

Too much.

I wasn't staying here in Mudville. I shouldn't have had to remind myself of that, especially since Declan was currently holed up in my attic apartment.

Glancing at Carson, I saw him watching me as I looked around the living room.

I smiled. "Nice place."

He rolled his eyes. "You can say it."

"Say what?"

"It doesn't exactly look like a typical bachelor pad."

I tipped my head to one side. "That's not necessarily a bad thing."

Back in Charlestown, when the guys I knew finally moved out of their parents' houses and rented an apartment, living room furniture usually consisted of a weight bench and video game console. Car magazines served as coasters. A roll of paper towels as napkins.

"This was my grandmother's house. She raised me here," Carson revealed, capturing all of my wandering attention.

At that moment I could actually feel my heart melt into a squishy, soft mass in my chest for the boy he'd been.

It was as if I could see that motherless child living here with his grandmother. Sitting at the card table that was covered in the plaid tablecloth and doing a puzzle there. Coming home from a boy scout meeting to have dinner and watch Jeopardy together on the sofa in front of what was probably then a big old television rather than the flatscreen there now.

All I wanted to do was wrap my arms around him and squeeze. Make him feel less lonely.

Carson shook his head. "Jesus. Kayleigh, you don't have to look at me like that. I'm not exactly a homeless orphan."

"No, you're not." But that didn't mean I still didn't want to hug him.

I closed the distance between us and pressed close. "Want to go to bed?"

"We didn't eat dinner yet." He glanced at the paper bag on the table.

He'd called in an order of wings from the bar and picked them up at the same time he picked me up.

"They'll keep. We can heat them up after."

His lips twitched as he reached up and ran his hand over my hair, brushing aside one curl that had fallen over my eye.

"After what?" he asked playfully.

"You know what." It was time I saw the bedroom and I couldn't wait.

I moved in for a kiss. He didn't argue.

27

CARSON

Kayleigh was sound asleep. Snoring softly. Rhythmically.

I smiled as I stood next to the bed, fully dressed, and watched her sleep.

Creepy? Maybe. But I was happy she was sleeping so well that she hadn't even stirred when I got out of bed and put on my clothes.

She didn't sleep at all usually, from what she'd told me, more than once. So that she felt comfortable enough here to be out like a light made me feel good.

I knew she wouldn't sleep forever. When she woke, I would be very happy to go for round two with her, after we finally got around to eating dinner. But to do that, I needed to get more condoms.

We'd blown through my stash. I hadn't realized until tonight I was down to the final one—which we'd already made very good use of. And although I wasn't at all opposed to getting creative and exploring other areas of pleasure, it was a situation easily remedied.

I would just run out to the store, grab a box, then be back here probably before she even woke and knew I was gone.

I'd already written a note so, in case she did wake, she wouldn't worry about where I was.

I eased the bedroom door closed and headed out.

It was that odd time of night where some stores were open and some had already closed. That was a reality of small town life. Even some of the gas stations closed at eight.

It usually didn't bother me. Tonight was a different story.

When I pulled up to the gas station closest to my house, the place I usually ran into when I needed one or two things, like milk or beer—or condoms—I found it dark.

I cursed beneath my breath. It looked like I was going to have to travel farther than I'd planned. Even so, it was only like five miles each way, so I sucked it up and hit the accelerator.

The route took me past the Muddy River Inn, and sap that I am, I couldn't help but glance fondly at the attic apartment above and remember the time I'd spent there with Kayleigh.

Until something had me hitting the brake.

A light had just gone out in her apartment. The

window had clearly been lit up. Now it was dark. As if someone had turned those lights out.

Kayleigh was at my place. So who was up there in her apartment?

I pulled my SUV slowly into the lot and parked next to her car.

My service weapon was locked in my dashboard. I reached to unlock the glove compartment. I grabbed a couple of plastic hand cuffs and my weapon.

I checked the clip and slapped it back in.

Damn right I was going in armed. We clearly had a trespasser and a petty thief in town. And unless Laney provided night-time cleaning service along with her apartment rentals, there was a good chance our suspect was up in Kayleigh's apartment.

The thought of a man breaking in while she'd actually been inside instead of at my place had my blood running cold.

Reaching beneath the seat, I grabbed my flashlight as well. I was as ready as I could be to take this guy down.

My adrenaline was pumping by the time I'd crept up the back stairs.

I needed the element of surprise. I couldn't knock. I didn't want to take the time to go downstairs and see if Laney had a spare key. Minutes could cost me the opportunity to grab this guy.

It took me about two seconds to decide to kick in the door. I'd pay to replace the lock.

Gun in my right hand, flashlight in my left, I raised my foot and thrust.

The door slammed against the wall as splinters of the broken door frame fell to the floor.

"Sheriff's department! Hands up!"

The beam of my light hit the face of a man. He looked to be a bit younger than me. Dark hair, a bit long as it curled around the collar of his T-shirt.

Eyes huge, hands up in the air, he said, "Don't shoot."

"Who are you and what are you doing in here?" I remained where I was, blocking what I knew to be the only exit to the apartment.

"I'm allowed to be here. The person who lives here invited me."

Those words made the world stand still.

I flipped on the light switch to get a better look at this guy and shoved the flashlight in the leg pocket of my cargo shorts. I did not lower the gun, however, even though every bit of law enforcement experience I had from my years on the force, everything I'd learned in training, seemed to drain from my brain.

All that was left was the question—who was this man to Kayleigh?

Was she cheating on me?

Now that I thought about it, it made sense why she'd pushed to come to my house tonight. She was hiding this guy at her place.

While I took much too long to respond to him, he

watched me. Waiting. But waiting like a pro. As if he was biding his time. Anticipating an opportunity to run when I let my guard down.

Now that I looked at him closer, he looked like a guy who'd maybe been at the business end of a gun before.

What I'd discovered in my investigation into Kayleigh's background hit me. The mob ties. My suspicion she was fleeing some trouble. Or someone.

What if that someone was this guy? What if she suspected she was being tailed and that's why she didn't want to be in her apartment tonight?

She hadn't even wanted to wait for me to pick her up upstairs. She'd made sure she was outside, right in front of the bar. A public place. Someplace she'd be less likely to be grabbed.

I was out of my league. We didn't have the mob in Mudville.

Playing it cool—or at least as cool as I could manage, I asked, "And whose apartment is this, who supposedly invited you?"

He paused. There was a definite delay during which I could see the decision process going on in his brain. He didn't know what to answer. Or maybe just didn't want to answer.

Finally, he said, "Kayleigh."

In spite of the pause, he delivered the correct answer.

"I'm going to have to check that out with her," I said, still suspicious.

If he were a bad guy here to do her harm, he wouldn't want me to ask her about him.

He surprised me when he lifted one shoulder. "Go ahead. She'll tell you."

Well, fuck. Now I was back to wondering if she had a personal history with this guy.

Maybe he was a boyfriend from her past who'd followed her here from where she used to live.

He sure wasn't from around here. I'd never seen him before.

Although, he did look oddly familiar. The dark wavy hair that stood out so much against his pale complexion. The shade of blue of his eyes.

Nah. I didn't know him. But he said that Kayleigh did, and I intended to ask her.

I pulled out my cell phone. I had to take my eyes off him briefly to navigate to my recent calls and hit her name to dial. But my eyes, and my gun, were both focused on him as I held the phone to my ear and listened to the ringing.

After about five rings, the call went to voicemail.

I guess it shouldn't be a surprise she hadn't answered. Her cell might be set on vibrate. And if I remembered correctly, it was currently in my living room. While she was most likely still asleep in the bedroom.

Now what?

If he were her boyfriend— Ugh. The word made me sick to my stomach with jealousy, but if he were, I didn't want to bring him down to the station. And if he were an invited guest, I couldn't arrest him.

But I couldn't be sure. Because he could just as easily have been sent by the mob to grab her...or worse. A hitman would know her name, as well as a friend.

It was too risky to not secure him.

Making a split-second decision, I said, "I'm going to cuff you. And then you're coming with me."

His eyes widened. "To the station?"

For a moment, I thought I saw fear flash across his features. Interesting.

"No. To see Kayleigh. Turn around."

He did as I asked and didn't fight me when I zip tied his hands together. I didn't carry my real handcuffs while off duty, but I always had some plastic ones in my car. Luckily, I'd grabbed a set of ties, just in case.

"Where are you taking me? Where is Kayleigh? She said she was going out with friends tonight."

"Oh, did she? Friends." I snorted at the word.

Yup. That lie made sense too. She didn't want one boyfriend to know she was going out with the other one. At least she was consistent and lying to us both.

Anger started to replace sadness and I took some satisfaction in saying, "She's at my place. In my bed."

His hands behind his back, he turned slowly to face

me, his eyes narrowing. "You're screwing my sister? Kayleigh's with a fecking pig?"

Sister?

For the second time that day, this man had managed to scramble my brain with a single sentence.

Meanwhile, the guy looked like he couldn't decide which to be more disturbed by. The fact his sister was in my bed. Or that I was *a pig*, as he'd so nicely put it. But I had more to worry about than having my profession insulted.

"Your sister?" I parroted.

That had been the last thing I'd expected him to say.

KAYLEIGH

There had been times when Carson had woken me in the most incredible and satisfying ways. This was not one of them.

Seeing my brother standing in the doorway of the bedroom in cuffs was not what I'd expected.

"Declan?" I'm sure I looked as shocked as I felt as I scrambled to cover my nakedness while figuring out how Carson had come to arrest my brother.

"You know him?" Carson asked, all cop. Gone was the gentle lover I'd fallen asleep next to.

"Yes. Of course, I know him." Still clutching the sheets to my chest, I glanced at Declan. He nodded, giving me the non-verbal okay to explain, "He's my brother."

Carson let out a visible breath. "Get dressed. We'll be in the living room."

He perp walked Declan back out of the room, but thank goodness he'd released his hands by the time I made it out, properly dressed, to where they were.

Declan was sprawled in the floral chair, his hands resting lightly on either arm, looking as casual as if he was waiting for a beer and the game to come on television.

Carson, on the other hand, stood stiffly, back ramrod straight, as he spun toward me.

"Why didn't you tell me your brother was here?" he asked.

"I didn't think it was important," I said as I perched on the edge of the sofa cushion.

Carson's brows shot up. He turned to Declan. "You wanna explain?"

Declan lifted one shoulder. "Explain what? I'm just visiting my sister."

"Why keep that a secret?" Carson asked, his frustration palpable.

After another shrug, Declan said, "Maybe she's embarrassed of her dear brother. Who knows?"

Pacing the room, from the old grandfather clock to the wall of family photos and back again, Carson let out an uncharacteristic string of obscenities before coming to stop in front of me. "I ran your car's plates, Kayleigh. I know where you're from. I know who your family is. And I know about their mob connections in Boston."

My license plate. Shit. I thought I was being so careful. I should have realized he could do that.

"I also know you're scared. I don't know of who or why. All I know is you're not telling me the complete truth. And I don't know why."

Declan snorted. "That's easy. It's because you're a cop."

"Declan. Hush up," I reprimanded.

"Is that really it?" he asked me directly.

Finally, I nodded.

That elicited another cuss. "I would hope by now, after all the time we've spent together, you'd know you can trust me."

Declan snorted again at that, earning him a glare from me.

"This thing is bigger than you, Carson. Bigger than us. Definitely bigger than this little town."

He paused, gaze leveled on me as he considered that. "So you're not going to tell me?"

I wished I could. But instead, I shook my head.

Carson drew in a deep breath and turned to Declan. "Things have been going missing around town. You know anything about that?"

"Me?" Declan's eyes grew comically wide, just like they used to when he was lying as a kid. "Nope. Nothing."

Jaw set, Carson said, "Don't suppose you know anything about the bones found at the Morgan place then either."

"Jaysus. What the feck is with all the questions about these bones? No. Hand to God, I've got nothing to do with any bones." Declan's gaze went from Carson to me and back again.

Carson, shoulders slumped, moved to the other end of the sofa and sat heavily.

"So what now?" I asked.

Carson let out a short humorless laugh. "What now, indeed."

"He's got no proof of anything, Kayleigh. No probable cause. Nothing. He has to let me go."

I eyed Carson. Glancing sideways, he noticed my gaze on him and said, "He's right. But that doesn't mean I won't be calling my counterpart in Charlestown and asking a few questions about Declan and Kayleigh Walsh." Carson shot Declan a warning glance.

Declan, cooler than I was, lifted one shoulder. "Knock yourself out."

I, not cool at all, said, "Please, Carson, don't do that."

Carson angled himself to face me. "Why not? Kayleigh, tell me. What are you two hiding?"

"Nothing," I answered.

He shook his head, looking disappointed in my answer.

At that moment, Declan decided to stand up. "Come on, Kay. Let's get out of here. He can't hold us."

Maybe not. But the last thing I wanted to do was leave Carson.

Not like this. Not with things so bad between us.

Then again, I had a feeling things between us would never be good again.

CARSON

In my defense, I managed to wait all the way until ten-thirty the next morning before I gave in, left my desk and drove over to the Muddy River Inn to talk to Kayleigh.

Her car wasn't there when I arrived. Heart speeding, I ran up the stairs and pounded on the door anyway.

She didn't answer. She could be out having breakfast with her brother. As much as I wanted to believe that, my gut instinct didn't agree.

Running out of options I went downstairs to the bar. Laney would be open early, as usual, serving coffee to the old timers and setting up the kitchen for the day.

She was there behind the bar restocking glasses when I pushed through the doorway.

"Hey, Laney. You know where Kayleigh is?" I asked.

Laney let out a huff. "No, but if you see her, tell her thanks a lot for leaving me short-handed on no notice."

"What do you mean?" I asked, a sick feeling creeping into my gut.

Laney tossed a handwritten note onto the bar. "I found that shoved under the door this morning. She left."

"Left? Is she coming back?" I asked, hoping, like an idiot, that she was maybe just driving her brother home to Charlestown and then she'd return.

"Doesn't look like it," Laney answered.

I reached for the note and after reading it, I had to agree.

She was gone for good and she'd taken her secret and her brother with her.

Meanwhile, against everything I knew I should do, I hadn't called the Boston Police this morning, in spite of my threat. I hadn't told anyone that I strongly suspected Mudville's petty thief had been in my custody and I'd let him go. And I had no intention of doing either because even now I was still blindly protecting Kayleigh.

I'd betrayed my oath to uphold the law. Compromised my integrity. And I'd still lost the girl.

Needless to say, this damn bachelor auction that had somehow snuck up on me and was happening tonight of all nights was the last thing I wanted to do.

Yet I had to do it.

I somehow made it through most of my day at work. But preparations for the auction started early in the afternoon and after fielding about a dozen phone calls from the committee, the sheriff told me to just leave work early and go over there.

So with my heart not in it, and no choice about the matter since it was basically an order from my boss, I headed over to the library.

I must not have been paying much attention at those many hours of meetings I'd endured since what I found there shocked me.

There was a full wooden stage, steps and all. As well as a sound system set up. Not to mention pop-up food and drink vendors.

This thing was bigger than I'd imagined...and I'd do anything to not be here.

Broken hearts needed bourbon and beer. Either while hanging out with the boys or alone in the dark. But this—this carnival atmosphere was not the cure for what ailed me.

Luckily the old biddies were all too busy fluttering around with last minute preparations to worry much about me and my hang-dog face.

Margaret Trout ordered me to carry some bags of ice for the lemonade to the bake sale table and then forgot all about me.

That left me free to go hide behind the stage and wait for the torture to officially begin.

It didn't take long for the other bachelors to discover my spot and join me there.

Their unhappy faces and grumbling helped. I guess it's true what they say. Misery does love company, even if my misery was Kayleigh-induced and theirs was just over having to suffer through this auction and the following dance.

The war stories started to come out as we all waited for the start of the auction.

Mister Timmerman began, grumbling about how Mary Brimley came over to rope his son Michael into being in this thing, and then proceeded to talk his ear off until he finally agreed to take part too.

Cash snorted. "That's nothing. Red is so mad at me for agreeing to be in the auction, she's refusing to come bid on me. So who the hell knows who is going to buy me."

Carter came skidding around the stage, looking flustered before he plopped down on the grass next to me.

"What's up with you?" I asked him.

"Laney's pissed. We're short-handed already and then I had to leave to come here."

"None of us are happy to be here, kid," Buck grumbled from where he perched on a rock wall.

"Oh, except for my mother being mad, I'm not unhappy to be here." Carter grinned as he rubbed his hands together. "I can't wait to see who bids on me."

Shit. I hadn't even thought about who might be bidding on me. Sadly, I couldn't muster the energy to care.

30

KAYLEIGH

I couldn't figure out how I'd ended up here. On the run from the mob with my brother the bank robber. And in love with a deputy who I'd left behind and would never see again.

The pain in my chest whenever I thought about leaving Carson was going to break me. I knew it.

As soon as I wasn't completely focused on saving Declan's life and figuring out how to feed and house us while still keeping us off the radar, I was going to fall apart.

For now, I'd cry if I weren't so numb.

We sat by the window in a booth at a diner just off the ramp at the Fort Drum exit on the highway. Across the street was a sign for a KOA campsite. Next door was a gas station.

Last night, after Declan and I walked back to my apartment from Carson's house, I'd thrown my few things in a bag, scribbled a note for Laney and pointed the car north.

I had all the cash I'd made while tending bar and I had a car. It was all we needed to flee. But having what we needed didn't make it any easier to leave.

It was pointless to think about what—make that whom—I'd left behind. I needed to be looking ahead.

I unfolded the map I'd bought at the gas station.

"I'm nervous about dealing with the border guards while crossing into Canada." I sighed. "I wonder if it would be smarter to smuggle you in by boat. Then I can drive the car over the border alone."

Glancing up I saw Declan's deep frown. "Kayleigh. I'm trying to avoid the mob. Not flee from the FBI or whatever. I don't think we have to worry about border guards."

"You don't think they..." I lowered my voice to barely a whisper, "can buy off the border guards? They definitely would and could."

"I hadn't thought that until you just said it." He scowled. "I don't think I need to leave the country anyway. They're not going to come looking for me all the way up here."

I glanced around. "I guess I could try to find work around here to support us."

"What is all this *us* and *we*? Kayleigh, wherever I end up, you're not coming. Thanks for the ride, but that's it. You're done. From here on out, I'm on my own. Go back to your life."

"No. Declan, I'm going with you—"

"No, Kayleigh, you're not. I ruined my life but I'm not going to let you ruin yours too. They're not looking for you. Go home. You're wicked smart. Put that degree of yours to good use. You worked so hard to get it."

I shook my head. "I'm not going to let you do this alone."

"Are you nuts? You actually have a future. You're the first one in our family to even go to college. Never mind to go for that fancy advanced degree. Don't throw it all away."

"Don't you throw *your* life away either. Turn yourself in. Ask for immunity in exchange for testifying against the others. Let them put you in witness protection."

Declan's eyes widened as he glanced around us. "Keep your voice down. And have you gone nuts? You want me to be a rat and trust the police?" He shook his head. "You were in Muddy Town too long. You forgot what it's like in the real world."

"No, I didn't—"

"You did. It's okay, Kayleigh. Can't say I blame you. That stupid little town had a certain charm to it. And I noticed you found one thing there *particularly charming*." He shook his head. "You and the deputy. Fuck me. That was the last thing I expected."

I felt the heat flood my cheeks. "Don't tease me." I didn't think I could handle it right now.

"Sorry. I just never thought I'd see you in love."

My head whipped up at the word. "Who said I'm in love?"

"You didn't have to say it. Neither did he."

I frowned. "Carson doesn't— He didn't say—"

Declan let out a short laugh. "You expect a lot from a man, Kay. He's not going to just come out and say it unless he's pretty damn sure you feel the same. You ever tell him?"

"No. Of course not."

"Then there you go," Declan said, shoving another french fry in his mouth.

I wasn't going to stay in Mudville. I wasn't supposed to fall in love. But Declan was right. I had anyway.

Declan reached out and laid his hand over mine. "You look exhausted, Kay. What do you say we grab a six-pack at the gas station, rent one of those cabins at the KOA and relax for the night? Regroup in the morning."

It was tempting. He was right. I was tired. More from the emotions than from the drive, but I was exhausted, nonetheless.

"I guess we drove far enough for today. Okay. Let's do it," I agreed.

Relaxing turned into me having one beer and immediately falling asleep, even though it was still daylight. I realized that when I woke up, found the sun still up and the cabin empty.

Declan was gone. But there was a note.

Gritting my teeth I read what he'd written.

I'll be fine. Don't worry about me. Don't come after me. And tell him how you feel! Also, call home so they know I'm okay.

My brat brother knew one beer would put me out. Especially after getting next to no sleep last night and after that long drive. This had been his plan to get away.

My anger turned into panic. What now? He was gone again, and I was in the middle of nowhere.

As I was debating what to do next, I realized he was right about one thing. I should call home. They deserved to know Declan was okay.

It was too risky to call my parents' house phone. But I knew Connor was smart enough to keep the cell phone he used for family off the mob and the police's radar.

I powered up my phone and hit to call his number.

"Kayleigh. About damn time you called."

"Nice to talk to you too, Connor. I found Declan."

"You did? Well, fuck me. Kay-bear, that's amazing."

"Don't get too excited. I lost him again. But he's good. Fine. Just stubborn."

Connor snorted. "Runs in the family."

I heard the insinuation in his voice. Yeah, I could be stubborn but so could he.

"Yeah. I agree," I tossed back with an equal amount of insinuation.

"Well, when you find him again you can tell him he can come home. The parties he was concerned about are no longer an issue."

"Wait, what do you mean there's no longer an issue?"

"Seems Liam and Seamus went for a swim and didn't make it out."

The men running the bank jobs mysteriously turning up dead right after threatening Declan was quite a coincidence.

"Connor," I began.

"Yes, Kayleigh?"

"Was it you?" I asked.

"Me? Never." His voice was too bright. Too cocky.

I wanted to believe him but I was having a real hard time. I'd bet if it wasn't him, he knew who it was.

"You going after him again?" Connor asked.

I sighed. "I wouldn't know where to start."

Unlike last time, I didn't have a clue of where he might have gone. He could have stolen a bike or a car. He could have hitched a ride. He could be over the Canadian border by now. Or halfway to Ohio for all I knew.

"So then come home."

I could but the thought of going back home to that life left me feeling cold.

Maybe I could try Boston. Or Amherst. I'd spent four years there during college.

Mudville. The word echoed in my head. I managed to keep it from coming out of my mouth.

"I don't know."

"Something's up with you. You sound different. What happened while you were gone?" Connor asked.

"Nothing." My knee jerk answer came out fast. But suddenly I didn't want to deny everything that had happened to me. "Can you keep a secret?"

Connor snorted out a laugh. "Me? Kay-bear. Come on."

"All right. Sorry. I know you can." Too well in my opinion. "So, I kind of met someone."

"Fuck me, Kay-bear is in love?"

I rolled my eyes as the second of my brother's was shocked by my actually having a love life for once.

"So who is he?" Connor asked.

This part was going to be trickier. "Um, he's kind of the deputy sheriff of the town where I was living while I looked for Declan."

"What the feck? Kayleigh Mary Elizabeth Walsh, you tell me you're joking right this minute."

"Wait. Before you flip out, I have to tell you, he let Declan go. He suspected he was on the run, definitely from the organization and possibly from the law as well. He suspected he'd been the one stealing to survive in the town where he was hiding and he let him go anyway."

"So he's in love with you."

Christ. It was like Connor and Declan were the

twins instead of Declan and me. They thought the same.

Still, I couldn't lie about this. "I don't know. Maybe?"

"Okay," he said.

"Okay?" I asked. What did that mean?

"Yeah. I'm okay with it. As long as he treats you right. And you know, it might not hurt to have someone on that side of the law in the family. But here's the big question. Is he Irish?"

I laughed. "I didn't ask. His last name's Bekker."

"Oh boy. There were no Bekkers in our town back home, I can tell you that. Ma and Pa might give you grief about him."

"Our parents giving me grief? What else is new? And it doesn't matter anyway. I snuck out of town without saying goodbye. He's not going to want to see me again."

"Don't be so sure. Go back. Apologize. Kiss and make up. He'll forgive you."

"You think?"

"I do."

Go back to Mudville?

Could I? Should I?

My heart pounded at the thought.

CARSON

Alice bid on Buck, who grumbled about it the entire time but looked secretly happy about the whole thing.

My fellow deputy John went to one of the ladies on the library board.

Red must really have been mad at Cash since she didn't even show up, even though her bestie Harper came. That was a surprise in itself knowing how Harper felt about the library and their anti-romance book stance. But then I saw Agnes and realized she'd accompanied her aunt.

Agnes ended up with the winning bid on Cash, thereby saving him from getting snatched up by one of the single women in town and causing real problems between him and Red.

The whole thing would have been amusing if I weren't so miserable.

In spite of my lack of enthusiasm, the auction continued on.

Stephanie, a friend who ran the animal shelter, bought Michael Timmerman, who I was pretty sure she was dating.

And in the shocker of the night, Mary Brimley bought Michael Timmerman's father, who did not look at all happy about it.

Stone's mother won old Jeb. Although the term *won* was questionable in this case. Her bid was the real act of charity of the event because no one else had bid on him. Not even when the opening bid dropped to ten bucks.

Finally, Carter and I were the last two men standing.

Carter went first and before I knew what was happening there was an all out bidding war for him. Cash and I stood on the sidelines, watching amazed.

"Who is that?" I asked, looking at the one girl who pretty much kept her paddle up. I recognized her but I couldn't come up with a name or how I knew her.

"She's the head of the cheer squad," Cash supplied.

That was why she looked familiar. I'd been to every home game of the season. My eyes widened as I realized the ramifications of what Cash had said.

"Wait. That means she's still in high school. Is she even eighteen? Are they allowed to bid that young?" I asked.

Cash frowned at me. "I don't know. You're the one who knows the law."

Charity bachelor auction law was out of my scope of knowledge. So I figured I might as well move on to the next question.

"Is that your cousin Shalene bidding against her?" I asked.

"Jesus. It is. Who's that third girl bidding?" Cash asked as the price for Carter rose above two hundred dollars.

The better question was where were they getting all this money to bid on Carter?

"I don't recognize her," I admitted.

I'd thought I knew everyone in town but I was wrong. These young girls all dressed and looked the same to me now that I was getting older.

The third girl finally won Carter for the grand price of two-hundred and ninety dollars. The highest bid of the night. An accolade which of course had him beaming.

"Did you see that?" Carter asked after climbing down from the stage. "It was crazy."

I had no comment and couldn't have stuck around anyway since now it was my turn. I left Carter with Cash and walked up the steps to the stage with as much enthusiasm as a man facing an executioner.

I stood next to Stone who, as mayor, was acting as the auctioneer.

He covered the mic and leaned toward me. "Ready?"

I shot him a sideways glance. "No."

"Better get ready." He lifted the microphone and said, "Now, last but not least, we have another member of Mudville's finest. Deputy Sheriff Carson Bekker. Who wants to start the bidding?"

"Twenty-five."

"Fifty!"

"Fifty-five."

They were supposed to bid in increments of ten dollars, but no one seemed to care about rules anymore. This thing had turned into a free for all. No one else had stepped up to stop the chaos, so I sure as hell wasn't going to be the one to do it.

The biddies looked thrilled they were bringing in so much cash for the library. Margaret Trout was keeping track of the bids while bent over a big ledger book like Scrooge McDuck. Meanwhile, I tried to see who was bidding on me.

The shouts were coming from all over the audience. A big enough crowd had gathered for the spectacle, that it was hard to make out any one person.

Finally, as the price reached two-hundred and forty-five dollars, I heard, "Three hundred!" shouted in a loud, clear voice that sounded oddly familiar.

I glanced at Stone and saw him react to the bid. That had me scanning the crowd to try and see who it had come from.

"Three hundred. Going once. Going twice. Sold to Harper Lowry for three hundred dollars."

He glanced at me and, wide-eyed, I stared back at him. "Harper?" I asked.

"Harper," he confirmed.

"Um. Sorry?" I said.

He laughed. "Don't worry about it. I'm just surprised, is all."

"You and me both," I agreed.

Stone turned back to the microphone and thanked the crowd and we were free to go find our dates for the night.

I definitely could have done worse than being won by Harper. If Stone was okay with this, I decided I had better be too. With Harper engaged to Stone, I figured saving me from one of the others was her act of charity.

I'd take it. The way I was feeling, I could use any help I could get.

Now, I suppose I had to find her. I spotted Agnes and headed that direction, figuring that was a good place to find her niece.

Cash was already over there and just behind me, Stone was heading in the same direction.

When I got closer the crowd parted enough I could spot Harper. I walked up to her, about to say thank you for saving me, when I saw her beam with a wide smile.

"Carson. Meet your date for the night." Harper

stepped aside to reveal tattooed skin, dark black hair and violet-blue eyes.

"Kayleigh?"

She looked a little unsure as she clasped her hands in front of her and said, "Hi."

My heart was pounding, but I managed to say, "Hi. Um, how?"

"Harper bid on you for me."

I cut Harper a glance and saw her glee, before I stepped up to Kayleigh. "I'm glad she did."

"Are you sure? I was afraid you wouldn't want to see me."

I saw the tears in her eyes and shook my head. "No. Never."

"I know we have to talk—" she began.

"We can do that later." I grabbed her hands in mine.

She nodded. "Okay. Later."

I pulled her against me and hugged her tight, kissing her on the forehead as she surreptitiously wiped away a tear.

Meanwhile the conversation went on around us. I was happy to let them all talk. For now, all I wanted to do was hold Kayleigh.

"Agnes, I want to thank you for winning me," Cash said.

The older woman let out a short laugh. "Don't thank me yet. You can repay me by coming over and fixing the rails on Petunia's pen. She's been leaning on them and cracked the wood."

"Well, she is turning into quite a beefy gal, Agnes," Cash commented.

"Cashel Morgan. Don't you dare fat shame Petunia." Planting a hand on her hip, Harper glared at him.

Cash drew back. "Jesus. You and Red spend too much time together. It's like you just channeled her and she spoke through you to scold me."

"To be fair. Petunia is a pig. She's not supposed to be skinny," Agnes pointed out.

Kayleigh pulled away far enough she could look at me. "Wait. Petunia is a pig?"

I nodded. "Yeah. She's Agnes's pet. She's also the Mudville High football team mascot."

"What? Wow. I had no idea. I'd heard she'd been kidnapped and just assumed…"

"Wait. Who did you think she was?" Harper asked, turning to join our conversation, which she'd obviously been listening to.

"One of the women in the detective society," Kayleigh said, looking a little embarrassed.

Cash busted out laughing. "That's hysterical."

Harper smiled. "That wasn't such a bad guess, I suppose."

Stone, who'd been waylaid by countless people on his way over, finally made it to us. He wrapped his arm around Harper and said, "That was a very nice thing you did."

"You mean giving money to my arch nemesis?"

Harper asked. "The same board of directors who insulted the entire genre of romance novels by refusing to have even one on the shelves in their esteemed century-old library?"

Stone smiled. "Yes, but also winning Carson for Kayleigh."

She smiled. "Oh, that. Yeah. It was worth it."

"Because they're so in *love*?" Cash asked making the word sound ridiculous the way he said it.

Harper nodded. "Yeah. And because I'm totally going to write that off as a charitable donation on my taxes and I got a great story idea out of it for a book."

"I had no doubt you would." Stone laughed.

Kayleigh, her cheeks pink, looked up at me. "I'm sorry about that."

"About what?" I asked.

"Them teasing us that we're in love."

"Don't be sorry. It's true. At least for me." I drew in a breath and asked, "What about you?"

She nodded, her eyes glassy with unshed tears. "Yeah. For me too."

My chest filled with what felt like a bubble of happiness that expanded until it spilled out of me in a huge grin that I could only control when I pressed my lips to Kayleigh's in a kiss that would have been better delivered in private.

Realizing where we were, I pulled back. But out of the corner of my eye I saw Stone reel in Harper and deliver a big kiss to her mouth too.

Kayleigh followed my gaze and said, "So, I guess we're going to end up just like them. And old happy couple."

I laughed. "Don't let Harper hear you calling them old. But as for ending up like them… Nah. I hope not. They're both great, but there's a lot of drama. I think I'm ready for a nice boring, drama-free life for a while. You?"

"Definitely. Drama-free will be a nice change." She sniffed out a short laugh. "Hey, you wanna get out of here?"

I wanted nothing more. But if I'd learned anything in those meetings it was that there was an iron-clad event schedule.

"We can't go yet. We have to dance first. And have our pictures taken for the paper."

Kayleigh cringed. "Pictures? In the newspaper?"

"Shit. I didn't think. You and Declan aren't safe yet, are you?"

She bobbed her head from side-to-side. "Maybe. I think we might be, but still…"

I shook my head. I'd just gotten her back. I wasn't going to take a chance on losing her again over some stupid photos in the local paper. "I'll pose for the picture with Harper. She's the winning bidder anyway. And besides, she'll love it. It'll be good for her Instagram."

"Then you'll take me home so we can be alone?" Kayleigh asked with so much heat in her gaze I almost said fuck it to the dance and the pictures and everything else except getting her alone.

"Baby, just try and stop me."

"Carson!"

Shit. What now? I turned and saw John Callahan heading my way.

"Yeah?"

"The sheriff just called. Oh, good. Stone. You're here too. Come on over. I got news."

Stone and Harper wandered closer. So did Cash and Agnes. "The call came in from the forensics team about the bones," John began.

"And?" Cash asked.

"They're definitely human but they're not new. In fact, he said they're likely very old. Decades old."

"Oh my. I know who's they are," Alice said, appearing from out of nowhere.

"You do?" Stone and Agnes spun to ask in unison.

Alice nodded. "It has to be Ted Simpson. Remember that couple who used to rent that old trailer that was parked along the river at your place?" she said to Stone.

He frowned and she shook her head.

"No, you wouldn't remember. Now that I think about it, this was years before your parents were even married. Well anyway, his wife caught him cheating."

Harper gasped. "So she killed him?"

"No. But he died. On top of the woman. In their bed. She came home and found him dead and the hussy running out the door with her girdle in her hand."

"So what did she do?" Cash asked.

"No one knew. All we knew was that there was never a funeral. Never a body seen by any of us. The local funeral home never got the body to embalm. And at that time, it was Agnes's house that was owned by the family who ran the funeral home out of it."

"Thanks for reminding me of that fun fact about the house where I sleep." Harper scowled.

"Some speculated she threw him in the river. But it was real dry that year. I don't think there was enough water in the old Muddy to hide a body."

"So you think she fed him to the pigs?" John asked.

"I do." Alice nodded.

John turned to Stone, while I stayed back with Kayleigh and let him conduct the questioning.

"That pig pen been there that long?" John asked.

"I don't know. Hang on." Stone glanced around and then shouted, "Jeb! Come over here."

It took a solid minute or two, but Jeb finally wandered over. "Yeah?"

"How long has the pig pen been on our property?" Stone asked.

"Built it myself when I was a young man working for your granddaddy," he answered.

"I think you have your answer," Agnes said.

"This is better than anything I could have made up." Harper started patting her pockets. "Where's my phone? I have to jot this down before I forget something."

Kayleigh looked up at me. "I don't think living in this town is going to be boring or drama-free."

Living in this town... She was staying. And that was all I needed to know.

I pulled her closer. "Nope. But you'll get used to it." And I'd be there to help her.

EPILOGUE

CARSON

"Carson!"

With a strong sense that I'd done this before, I turned away from the door of the Muddy River Inn and walked down to Mary Brimley's car. Except this time, instead of Alice Mudd hanging out of the car, it was Margaret Trout.

"Yes, ladies?" I asked as a crisp autumn breeze put enough bite in the air I was grateful for the warmth of the noon-day sun.

I was meeting Kayleigh for lunch here, so I was both hungry and anxious to get inside to see her. But since there wasn't another centennial celebration coming up any time soon, I felt confident I was in the clear to talk to the ladies on my way in.

"We wanted to know if you'd consider being a guest speaker at our next Ladies Amateur Detective Society meeting."

"Me?" I asked. "Don't you want the sheriff instead? He has much more experience."

I wasn't above throwing my boss under the bus. I didn't feel an ounce of guilt over it either. He'd do the same to me.

Margaret waved away my suggestion. "Goodness no. We want you."

Mary leaned across the car, almost laying in Margaret's lap so she could join the conversation. "You're younger and more handsome. We'll have a much larger crowd if we advertise you're the guest speaker."

"Um. Okay. Sure. I'll do it. No problem. But you'll have to excuse me now. I have someone waiting inside."

"The meeting is at three o'clock in the bar a week from Tuesday," she said as I turned to walk away.

"Got it. Thanks," I called back while still walking.

Inside, Kayleigh wasn't at our usual table. Instead, she was behind the bar.

Frowning, I slid onto a barstool and asked, "What are you doing back behind the bar?"

She and Laney had made up and Kayleigh was renting the upstairs apartment again, but she wasn't working here anymore. She'd gotten a job as a guidance counselor at the college twenty minutes away.

"Laney had to run downstairs and help a customer in the liquor store. But the girl she hired to replace me is running late, so I told her I'd watch the bar for a few minutes."

"That was very nice of you," I said.

"I was feeling generous. Declan called." Her smile lit up her face.

"Oh, baby. I'm so glad. I know you've been worried. What did he have to say?"

"He joined the Army," she announced, looking as surprised as I was.

"Really? That's unexpected."

"You're telling me." She sniffed.

"How do you feel about that?"

She bobbed her head. "I'll worry. Of course. But you know, I think it might be good for him. Now he has purpose. A place. I think that's what he needed."

"Good. I'm glad." If she was happy, so was I. "So, what do you want to do tonight?"

"Maybe Chinese food and a movie at your place?" she asked.

"Sure. That sounds good." At least, most of it sounded good.

I was starting to hate that there was a *my place* and a *her place*. But I was hoping to change that soon.

After three months of dating, I knew we were moving fast, but I didn't care. I was going to ask her if she wanted to move in with me.

Maybe I'd even stop by the hardware store and get a key cut.

Then I could pop into Red's shop and see if she had

a fancy keychain or maybe a cute little trinket box I could put it in.

I could give it to Kayleigh tonight. I liked that idea. With any luck, so would she.

"Oh, there's one more thing," she said, grinning.

"What's that?" I asked, curious.

"Don't make it obvious, but look at the corner table."

I did my best to not look obvious as I casually glanced around the bar, not knowing exactly what I was looking for. Until I saw it.

I spun back to face her. "Is that old Buck and Alice Mudd on a date?"

"It is. Her friends were already in here spying on the whole thing. Nice to know they spy on one of their own as much as they do us. Margaret had to get home or they'd still be here. In fact, it wouldn't surprise me if Mary dropped Margaret off and came back."

I couldn't help but smile as I took another look at the old couple. "Good for them."

"I agree." She nodded. "I think it's nice they found each other. We should only be so lucky to be like them when we're their age."

"You think we might be like them when we're their age?" I asked.

"I hope so. Don't you?"

I did. But agreeing didn't seem like enough. And before I knew what was coming out of my mouth, I blurted, "Move in with me."

"What?" Kayleigh laughed.

"I want you to move in with me. If that's what you want." So much for my big plan for tonight.

She smiled, then nodded. "Yes. It's what I want."

My grand romantic gesture was back on. I'd present her the key at my place over Chinese food, just like we'd eaten on our first date.

Tonight would be the first night of the rest of our lives together.

DOG DAYS

1

STEPHANIE

Here's the thing about small towns. Everyone knows everyone else. And, what's really annoying, is that everyone knows everyone else's business.

So it really shouldn't have been a surprise to find the deputy sheriff standing in front of me at the animal shelter, barely fifteen minutes after I started my shift.

Why the deputy was here was no mystery. It could only be about one thing. This morning's incident.

In spite of my certainty, I chose to play dumb. "Good morning, Carson."

"Stephanie." He tipped his dark blonde head to me with as much authority as he could given the fact that, with my being seven years his senior, I'd been his babysitter once upon a time.

I folded my arms and waited, pretty confident he

wasn't here to arrest me. Although in this town, you never knew. Mayor Pickett and the town council could have passed any sort of ordinance at one of their many, many town meetings . . . I really needed to start attending those.

"So, the reason I'm here," Carson begin. "Mr. Timmerman—"

He didn't have to go any further. It was just as I'd suspected. And completely ridiculous.

I held up one hand to interrupt him. "Can I explain my side of the story, please?"

Carson's brows rose. "All right."

I couldn't believe that freaking old man had really called the sheriff's department on me. For one little pile of dog poop!

Okay, maybe not so little. Zeus, as a Belgian Shepherd, left pretty large piles, but I always picked up each and every one. Until today.

"I was walking Zeus. He, you know, did his business, and that's when I discovered I was out of plastic bags. So I ran across the street to Red's Resale shop and got one from her. Carson, seriously, I was literally gone for like two minutes. Maybe three, tops. But by the time I got back, the poop was gone. Tell me, what was I supposed to do?"

"Look, Steph, I believe you. But my hands are tied here. An official complaint was made."

I sighed. "Fine. What do I need to do to make this right?"

Pay a fine? Spend a day on the rack in the town square?

The scary part was, here in Mudville, New York, a village with barely over a thousand residents—that last scenario wasn't out of the realm of possibilities.

No, we didn't actually have a rack, but I was sure some of the crotchety old residents would swarm to the next meeting to vote to approve it if a proposal for one was on the agenda. I included Mr. Timmerman in that grouping.

Carson drew in a breath, his chest expanding beneath the short-sleeved khaki shirt of his deputy's uniform. "Mr. Timmerman says he'll let it drop if you apologize."

"Apologize?" I repeated. Of all my guesses, that wasn't one of them.

He nodded. "Yup."

"Like a written apology?" I asked, hopeful I'd get away without having to see the man.

Carson shook his head. "He said, and I quote, *if she gets her* uh," his gaze cut to mine and then away as he clearly edited what old man Timmerman had said, "*self over here today and apologizes, I'll let it go*. And then he reminded me he eats promptly at five and that he doesn't like to be disturbed during his dinner."

I drew in a breath, trying not to be angry or annoyed by reminding myself that I was getting off easy with just an apology rather than a fine.

Make that *another* fine since I'd already had to pay

fifty dollars for the sin of not getting a dog license for Zeus. Never mind that I was just fostering him at my house because he wasn't doing well in the cage alone overnight at the shelter.

It didn't seem to matter to the animal control officer that the dog was a veteran who'd served his country for years in the war zone, as well as only a temporary resident in my home.

"All right. I'll apologize." I glanced behind me. Terri was on today with me. "I'll go over on my lunch hour."

Wouldn't want to risk disturbing Mr. Timmerman's insanely early dinner by waiting until after work.

"That would be great. Thank you," Carson said with sincerity.

I scoffed. "Why are you thanking me? You're the law, remember? All I'm doing is complying with an official order."

He treated me to a small, almost sad-looking smile. "Yes, but there are those in this town who wouldn't have agreed to comply so easily. So thank you for making my life a little easier."

Good chance Carson was referring to Red, who was as fiery as her hair color, and how she'd either saved—or stolen—a calf from the stock auction. The story changed depending on who you talked to, but I'd heard it was poor Carson who had responded to the auction owner's complaint.

I smiled at Carson's obvious exasperation with small town law enforcement. "Sure. Anytime."

I'd comply. No problem. It didn't hurt to have the gratitude of the local lawmen for the next time I did something horrible—at least, horrible by small town standards—like jaywalking or neglecting to bring in my garbage pail from the curb in a timely manner. Or, you know, something else equally nefarious.

When Carson had left, looking grateful to be done with me and the case of the unscooped poop, I asked Terri if she'd mind if I took an early lunch today.

I decided to get this slap on the wrist over with sooner rather than later. I also decided to bring Zeus with me. One, it was his poop that had started all this.

And two, horrible though it sounded, I wasn't above rubbing Zeus's veteran status in the old man's face. Just to make him feel a little guilty for bitching about a mess that I had been going to clean up myself *if* he'd just given me the chance.

I was less grateful about my light sentence and was becoming good and annoyed again by the time I pulled my car in front of old man Timmerman's house.

On the village's Main Street, lined with large and stately Victorians, the single level ranch-style house sat firmly in their shadow, both literally and figuratively.

Squinting at the property through narrowed eyes, I

took note of everything wrong with it. Things I'd overlooked before when I'd been just walking by.

The grass was long and needed cutting. Weeds grew tall beneath the overgrown bushes flanking the front door. The house's paint job had seen better days—just like the old man himself, I supposed.

Humph. Maybe he should pay a little extra attention to things closer to home and worry less about one little—okay, not so little—pile of crap by the curb.

I drew in a bracing breath and got my thoughts together, rehearsing my apology before I went to the door.

There were plenty of things I wanted to say to this man, but I curtailed my comments to the bare necessities—a short and sweet apology—actually, drop the sweet part and make that just a *short* apology.

Once I had my wording right, I glanced at Zeus, perfectly behaved as he rode shotgun in the passenger seat, as usual.

He was a very good passenger. I was told he even knew how to parachute out of planes from his military days so I guess riding in a car was no challenge for him.

"You ready, buddy boy?" I asked.

He wagged his tail.

Now that he wasn't depressed from being stuck in a shelter cage all day and night, he was always excited for an adventure.

Depending on how old man Timmerman reacted to my apology, this could turn into quite an explosive adventure. That was okay. Zeus was trained for explosions too.

After procrastinating as long as I could, I got out of the car, my feet dragging, along with the end of Zeus's leash in my grasp.

I made my way up the short staircase to the small porch outside the front door with about as much dread as a person going in for a root canal.

Not a surprise. This might end up being that painful.

I pushed the doorbell, which looked to be from about the nineteen-fifties. I didn't hear it ring inside. I pushed again, listening more closely this time.

Still nothing.

Crap.

That figured. The old man demanded an apology in person, but he didn't have the decency to have a working doorbell.

Annoyed, I raised my fist and pounded on the door. I continued to pound, hard and loud, determined that I'd make him hear me even if I walked away with bruises on my fist.

"Hang on! Dammit." The annoyed though muffled male voice halted my fist mid-pound and started me reconsidering the wisdom, or rather foolishness, of pissing off this man further.

Too late now.

I heard the clicking of the lock and then the door was yanked open. But it wasn't old man Timmerman on the other side.

Oh, no. Far from it.

This man was one fine specimen of ripped muscles and shirtless wonder.

My gaze dropped all the way down to the happy trail that disappeared beneath the waist of his low-slung jeans, the button and belt of which was undone and hanging open.

He was barefoot as well, or at least his left foot was bare. His right foot was gone.

When I realized I was staring at the missing appendage, I yanked my gaze up.

The face was older, and a whole lot angrier, but I recognized him. Mudville High's Class of 1998 football star and all-round bad boy Michael Timmerman.

I had been a freshman when he was a senior, but I still knew him. Everyone did.

Truth was, I more than knew him. I'd had an epic though unrequited crush on this guy for my entire freshman year, through the summer and halfway into my sophomore year, when I realized he'd left town and, when Christmas came and went without a visit, he likely wasn't coming back.

He was the guy who graduated high school and then, a week later, disappeared, never to be seen again. During that week, he attended a few keg parties and made his mark by out-drinking everyone and sleeping with half the cheer squad, all in between kicking anyone's ass who looked at him sideways.

I'd heard he joined the military. A shock in itself given his propensity for debauchery and breaking the rules.

If he visited his dad during the past twenty years, I hadn't known about it. But now he was back. The reason why was obvious. My gaze dropped again to his missing foot before I yanked it back up.

He leaned heavily on the doorframe, balancing on his one leg, glaring at me with all the fire of hell flashing in his eyes.

"What?" he demanded.

Startled, I jumped at the question that had been blasted at me in a sharp, ominous tone. It was the kind of voice I imagined commanders used on recruits in boot camp. Not the kind of voice one used to answer the door in Mudville.

Zeus whined next to me, no doubt sensing my discomfort. "Um, hi. I'm Stephanie, from down the street. Is your father around?"

"No." He leaned back, about to close the door on me.

"Wait. I'm sorry, but he told me to come by. Well, actually, Carson did." I realized Carson was still a child when this guy had left and added, "He's a deputy in town."

Michael drew in a deep breath—and I did my best to ignore the rise and fall of his muscles.

"Why?" he asked.

Apparently, he was fond of one-word sentences. With the amount of vitriol with which the single word was delivered, his keeping it brief was fine with me.

My heart pounding, I had to think quick. I knew he had little patience with me, which meant I only had a short time to speak. "Zeus pooped on your lawn and I didn't have a bag and your father saw me not pick it up and called the sheriff's office and said I had to apologize today or I'd be in trouble."

I delivered the one long sentence in a single breath, hoping to get it all in before he slammed the door in my face.

As it was, I wasn't sure I'd get credit for my apology. I'd have to come back again later. That was the last thing I wanted to do, even if the view was a nice one.

At least the view from his neck down was.

Oh, no doubt, Michael was a ruggedly handsome man. But his expression turned him from sexy to just plain scary.

My heart pounded as I awaited his response. But he didn't speak. He did the last thing I expected. He started to laugh, finally wiping his hand over his face to control himself enough to say, "So that's what the old man was storming around the house about."

"I only ran across the street to Red's to get a bag to

pick it up. But by the time I got back, it was gone. I never meant for him to have to clean it up. I swear," I explained further, hoping he'd see my side and advocate for me with his father.

He shook his head. "He didn't clean it up. That lady who lives next door picked it up and then came knocking to tell him she did."

My eyes widened. "Mary Brimley? Mother fucker," I spat.

It had to have been her since she lived next door. As the self-appointed town gossip, she was the first to report anyone not toeing the line in this town.

Red's friend Harper had started calling her Binoculars Brimley because she saw everything. Damned if today didn't prove that.

So *she* was the one who'd seen Zeus. She was the one who tattled. If it weren't for her, I would have had the poop cleaned up before old man Timmerman ever saw it and none of this would have happened.

I glanced up to find Michael smirking. I realized I'd just cussed like a sailor and cringed. "Sorry about my language."

He scoffed. "Don't be sorry on my account."

I blew out a breath, unsure what to do. "Do you know when your father will be home?"

"He went to the store. But that usually entails a side trip to the bar so I wouldn't expect him home any time soon."

"Oh." Deflated, I sighed. "I guess I can come back."

"Look. You don't have to apologize. I'll let him know you were here. And I'll tell him what happened."

"Will that make him happy?" I asked.

He lifted one dark brow above eyes so deep and intensely blue I momentarily fell into them, only just pulling myself out before I drowned. "Nothing makes him happy. But yeah, it should keep you out of trouble."

"That would be great. Thank you."

"No problem."

"And um—" I almost thanked him for his service. But it seemed too trite. The man had given a limb. At a loss I finally said, "It's good to have you back in town."

Stone-faced, he leveled a dark glare on me. "Glad you think so."

With that, he hopped backward once, then again, and then the door I'd been expecting to be slammed in my face since my arrival was just that.

I stood a second, thrown by the encounter. Finally, I glanced down at Zeus to see how he'd handled the interaction. We'd noticed at the shelter he didn't like loud noises or raised voices.

After what he'd been through, who could blame him?

I could see he hadn't liked how our visit had ended any more than I did. There was concern evident in his dark brown doggy eyes.

It seemed they were both wounded warriors—Zeus and Michael. Some wounds were on the outside, but there were many more invisible ones on the inside.

Still, they were wounds nonetheless. And wounds could be healed.

A thought hit me. And idea that had my heart racing.

I'd managed to help Zeus. He'd been in bad shape, emotionally, when he'd first arrived. I'd gotten him out of his depression. I'd made real strides in helping him acclimate and become more social.

If I could do it for Zeus, couldn't I do the same for Michael Timmerman?

Maybe. Maybe not. People and dogs weren't all that different, but they weren't all that similar either.

All I knew was, I sure as hell was going to try.

2

The next day dawned sunny and unseasonably hot. Odd for autumn in this region but not unheard of. After a lifetime here I'd learned to expect snow in May and heat in October.

Consequently, I didn't put my winter clothes away until July and kept my summer outfits out through the start of November.

I pulled out a pair of knee-length shorts and one of my short-sleeved T-shirts from the animal shelter to wear for today, along with a pair of sneakers.

Zeus liked to walk fast in the morning after a good night's rest. I needed to be dressed appropriately.

After coffee and a fried egg for me, and a bowl of food and water for Zeus, we set off on what had become our morning ritual. It encompassed a two-mile walk from my house on Depot Street, to the other end of Main Street where all the businesses where located.

There, we'd turn around and come back again.

It was the same every day. Except this morning, I found myself slowing as I passed the Timmerman house. Watching the windows for signs of life inside now that I knew Michael was back.

How long had he been home? Chances were good the reason I didn't know was because he hadn't left the house since returning.

That was going to change.

I picked up my pace and Zeus matched my speed as we made a beeline to the bakery. Honey Buns was already open since it attracted the early morning coffee and pastry crowd.

Perfect.

I looped Zeus's leash onto the hook provided right outside the bakery and bent to pet him. "I'm going to be right inside here for one minute. Then I'll be back. Okay?"

He laid down and rested his head between his paws. I took that as a *yes* and strode inside.

There I found Bethany sliding a tray of her signature pastry onto a shelf in the glass display case.

She straightened, giving me a view of her "Honey Buns—We'll Leave You Sticky" T-shirt.

"Good morning, Stephanie" she greeted. "What can I get for you today?"

"G'morning, Bethany," I replied. There were some

amazing looking things in the case. Cupcakes, cookies, even a pie, but I had a plan. "Can I have four honey buns boxed to go, please?"

"Sure thing." She smiled. "Any coffee?" she asked.

As good as the fresh-brewed coffee smelled, I knew I couldn't handle Zeus's leash and a box of pastries and a coffee so I shook my head. "Very tempting, but I can't today. I'll stop in again tomorrow."

"Sounds good." She nodded and rang up my total on the vintage register.

I paid with the cash I always tucked into my pocket before our walk and thanked her, grabbed my box and stepped outside.

Part one of my plan complete, I grabbed Zeus's leash from the hook and he and I made our way back up Main Street toward home. Or, more accurately, toward the Timmerman house.

I paused at the end of the sidewalk that led to the front door.

Just as I was steeling my nerves to knock on that door and risk the wrath of one or both of the Timmerman males, I heard a lawnmower start. Or at least try and fail to start.

I also heard the accompanying obscenities at the failure. Then finally, the steady buzz of the engine got louder until the riding mower, and the man driving it, came around the corner of the house and into view.

Michael was in a tank-top today rather than

shirtless, but his bulging biceps were still on full display. But in spite of the heat he wore long pants.

I noticed he was operating the machine with his right leg. The leg with the missing foot.

My gaze dropped to the prosthetic he hadn't been wearing yesterday. I pulled my gaze up as he drove straight at me, braking just in time to avoid running me over.

He cut the engine and glared with those blue eyes that would have been breathtaking if they didn't project such annoyance.

His dark brows low, he said, "Yes?"

"Hi," I greeted brightly, hoping my good mood would counteract his bad one.

"Hi." Those brows rose but his tone remained flat.

"I, uh, brought you and your dad some honey buns from Bethany's."

"Why?" After the third one-word sentence in a row I had to give him credit for remaining consistent.

I lifted one shoulder. "I don't know. Just being neighborly. Consider it a welcome home."

He shook his head. "How do you even know me?"

"I was a freshman when you were a senior."

He cocked up one brow. "Forgive me if I don't remember you."

No surprise there.

Chances were good I was painting sets for the school play while he was out on the football field practicing. Or, more likely, in the backseat of his car practicing something else on one of the cheerleaders.

"That's fine. It wasn't like we ran in the same circles or anything." I laughed. He didn't. "So anyway. Here."

I thrust the bakery box at him. He stared at it from his seat on the lawn tractor and I realized he had nowhere to put it if he took it from me.

"Or I could run it up to the porch and leave it there for you," I suggested.

"Yeah. Do that."

Why did I imagine he'd edited out the word *idiot* from the end of that sentence? If so, I'd just count myself lucky that he had left it unspoken.

"All right. I'll just do that then. Come on, Zeus." We trotted up to the front stairs and left the box on the top step, before turning around and heading back.

He watched, unmoving, unsmiling.

"So, uh, enjoy." I delivered a small wave and pivoted for the street, intent on getting away from there. And away from his stare, which looked half baffled, half annoyed.

"Hey!" The sound of his voice stopped me.

Uh, oh. Was I in trouble? I turned. "Yeah?"

"Thanks."

It was only one word, and it was delivered with the same lackluster tone, but it was civil and courteous and so unexpected and welcome that I couldn't help but smile.

"You're welcome." I tugged Zeus down the road before Michael saw me grinning like a lunatic, all over one little *thanks*.

But it was more than that uncharacteristic display of common polite courtesy. Michael was out of the house. Making an effort to take care of the property.

Slowly but surely, he was coming out of his shell. He'd come around eventually. I was sure of it.

I was calling phase one of this plan a success. Tomorrow, on to phase two. I couldn't wait.

3

The following morning was no less stifling nor was I any less nervous for the next phase of my plan. But I was nothing if not determined.

Zeus in tow as both my inspiration and my motivation, I waltzed directly up to the front door and knocked, before my nerves could get the better of me.

I'd been worried about what Michael would think of my being here again with nothing but the flimsy excuse I'd rehearsed to explain my presence.

What I should have been concerned about was the possibility that Michael might not be the one to answer the door.

When the door opened, there was Michael's father, standing in the opening, glaring at me with the same expression as his son had.

"What?" he asked.

Now I knew where Michael got his conversational skills.

I smiled as sweetly as I could. "Hi, I was looking for Michael."

His graying brows drew down over bloodshot blue eyes. "Why?"

"I got it, Pops."

I'd never been so relieved to hear that grumpy voice in my life.

Old man Timmerman looked about as confused as he could be, but he moved to the side, and then Michael was there.

Momentarily struck dumb, I stood silent and took in how his dark hair looked even darker wet, I guessed from the shower since he was also shirtless.

At least he had been, until he pulled on the T-shirt he'd held in his fist. Before he did though, I'd gotten an eyeful of some pretty nice pecs. And just the briefest glimpse of a fine mesh of scarring covering his right side.

"Good morning," I said, happy I could get any words out at all.

"Good morning," he repeated.

I wondered if he'd always repeat my greeting. Maybe tomorrow I'd begin with *top of the morning to ya* and see what he said.

Ignoring that I might not be welcome here tomorrow—or today for that matter—I forged ahead with my plan.

"So, I was wondering if you could do me a favor."

There went that brow again, up, up and away. "What kind of favor?" he asked.

Zeus, don't fail me now.

I glanced down at the dog, about to use him for a prop. Though, given the circumstances, I didn't think he'd mind.

"It has to do with Zeus here," I began.

I braced myself for the next part, which would either get me thrown off the property or deliver exactly what I wanted. That being Michael.

Er, I meant *Michael coming out of his shell.* I wasn't here trying to get the man for my own pleasure. Of course not.

"Zeus has been displaying some behavioral issues since he arrived at the shelter. He's comfortable with me now, but he still doesn't like being around a lot of people or other dogs. It's why I bring him home with me every night after work."

"You work at the shelter?" he asked, shocking me that he'd taken the initiative to ask me a question. That he was interested in knowing the answer.

"Yes." I nodded. Encouraged, I went on. "Anyway, I did some research online and apparently his behavior is typical of canine PTSD. But I think it's more than that. I think part of the problem is he misses his handler."

A change swept over Michael's features. "He's a military dog?"

"Yup. They retired him after he was injured overseas." I held my breath as I waited to see how he'd react to that.

His nostrils flared as his breathing quickened. Finally, he asked, "What do you think I can do for him?"

"I thought maybe you could come on his walk with us. We only go to the stores down the block and then back."

His gaze dropped while I forced mine not to and braced myself for his no. Wearing a prosthetic while walking down Main Street of the town where he had once been the star athlete had to be tough.

I knew nothing about his situation or even these kinds of injuries in general.

How recent was the injury? Was he completely healed or did he have more to go? Did it hurt him to walk? Would he have a noticeable limp or not?

I realized, too late, I was interfering where I shouldn't be—

"Okay."

My head whipped up at his answer. "Okay?"

"Let me just tell my father I'm going out."

"Of course. Sure. I'll be right here."

He delivered a single nod and then closed the door as I stood dumbfounded.

Was my plan actually working? I glanced down at Zeus—the miracle dog who'd survived the explosion that had killed his handler, but they had saved the rest of his unit.

He might be officially retired, but there was at least one more soldier he could help.

"Your service isn't finished yet, buddy," I whispered, bending down to pet his head.

The door opened again and I jumped to stand up straight. "Ready?" I asked.

"Yeah," he said, back to the single word sentences.

That was fine. We didn't have to talk. He was outside and walking. That was good enough.

Zeus, of course, was thrilled to have the additional company.

I took it slow, since I wasn't sure how fast Michael could move. Good boy that he was, Zeus meandered as slowly as we did, taking the time to sniff everything we passed and pee on a few choice things.

"What will happen to him?" Michael asked.

"We're going to try to find him a forever home."

Michael frowned. "Why don't you keep him?"

I let out a short laugh. "If I kept every animal I fostered, I'd need an ark."

The truth was I'd already considered keeping Zeus . . . until I'd seen Michael standing in the doorway of his father's house. That's when I knew they needed each other.

Meanwhile, Michael was still frowning. Apparently, he hadn't liked my little ark joke.

"If the perfect person doesn't come along for him, I'll adopt him officially myself," I added.

The frown softened with Michael's nod. I guess that was the correct answer.

We'd reached Bethany's shop and instead of turning around to go back, I faced Michael. "Come inside."

The frown returned. "I didn't bring my wallet."

"You don't need a wallet. My treat," I offered.

The frown deepened. He might not say much but at least his face was expressive. His eyebrows in particular.

I forged ahead. "You can stay out here with Zeus if you want while I run in. What do you take in your coffee?"

He scowled but finally said, "Black."

"Eww. Really? No, come on. Tell me for real. What do you want in the coffee?"

He laughed. "That is for real. Black. No sugar."

Afraid he wouldn't ever laugh again if I made a big deal out of it, I tried not to react to the fact that I'd actually gotten that laugh out of him.

Instead, I wrinkled my nose in playful displeasure and said, "Ugh. Okay. Whatever you want."

I hopped up the stairs and pushed through the doorway, ready to kill Michael with kindness—and a bag of sweets to go with it.

A couple of minutes later I came through the doorway with my hands filled with a bag containing two honey buns and two coffee cups. I found Michael had made himself comfortable in one of the chairs set up outside. And Zeus had settled right in with him, sitting on the grass while leaning up against Michael's leg.

I couldn't have asked to find anything better than this. I bit my lip to suppress my smile and strode to the table.

"Icky coffee. Black, no sugar. And a honey bun, containing lots of sugar, I'm sure."

He rolled his eyes, but said, "Thanks."

Attitude aside, Michael dug right into his honey bun and his coffee.

Looking back over his shoulder he said, "This place wasn't around when I lived here."

"No, it wasn't." I laughed. "Because Bethany was probably about eight when you left town. It was a coffee shop already though, before she took it over. But before that, I can't remember what was here. Some sort of office, I think."

He lifted one shoulder. "Things change."

"Yup," I agreed.

Looking around while sipping at my own coffee with cream and sugar, I spotted Alice Mudd and Mary Brimley coming out of the diner across the street.

Mary almost fell off the bottom step, she was so busy watching me and Michael rather than where she was stepping.

Still pissed about her tattling on me about the poop

incident, I scowled. "And yet some things always remain the same."

He followed my gaze and snorted out a laugh. "There's your favorite person."

"Yes. Maybe I'll drop off a gift for her. Zeus hasn't pooped yet today."

Michael choked on the coffee he'd been swallowing during my ill-timed comment. I pressed my hand to my mouth. "Oh, my God. Sorry."

He shook his head and finally recovered. "It's all right."

His voice sounded slightly gruffer than usual. And oh so sexy. It might be worth making him choke again just to hear the sultry timbre of it.

After the gossip crew had moved on we sat in silence. Michael stared into the distance, seeming at ease. Relaxed.

Absently, he rubbed the back of Zeus's neck with one hand as he sipped his coffee with the other.

I couldn't help my smile. It was my small version of a victory lap, until he said, without even looking directly at me. "Stop."

My smile faded. "Stop what?"

"Stop staring at me while looking so pleased with yourself." He finally turned his gaze toward me. "I would have gotten into town eventually, *without* your interference."

He was perceptive, seeing right through my ruse. I'd have to remember that.

"Mmm. Probably. But you wouldn't have had as much fun." This time I didn't control my grin.

The best part was, he couldn't either. Shaking his head, he covered his own crooked smile by taking another sip of coffee, but I still saw it. And that was good enough for me.

Phase two was a success. Onward. I couldn't wait.

4

I noticed I was starting to look forward to my long walks with Zeus to the exclusion of all else. As if I was only suffering through the day at a job I truly did love usually, just so I could go home and set out for Zeus's walk on Main Street.

In past, I'd walk Zeus toward town in the mornings and away from town, toward the river in the evenings. I enjoyed the change in the view.

So did Zeus, which was probably why he looked at me so strangely this evening when I pulled him in the opposite direction.

Yes, I was breaking our tradition in hopes that I could see Michael for a second time today. But Zeus wouldn't understand that.

Or maybe he would. As we neared the Timmerman house, he picked up speed. When he saw Michael sitting on the small front porch, his tail started wagging. And when I broke the holy Mudville leash law and dropped my hold to let him run, Zeus sprinted toward Michael.

By the time I reached the two, Zeus had both paws on Michael's knees and was wiggling with happiness as Michael rubbed his head with both hands.

"Sorry about him. He pulled away from me."

Michael glanced up, doubt in his gaze. I guess he'd seen me drop the leash and let Zeus go. Although he didn't comment on it. Instead, he said, "He's fine.

It was hot as hell this evening, definitely shorts weather, but I noticed Michael had on long pants. I had to assume it was because he wasn't ready for anyone to see his prosthetic.

In fact, I was pretty sure he was happy not seeing people at all.

I could arrange *chance* meetings between him and Zeus until he realized he needed the dog in his life, but I had no clue what to do about his retreating from society.

What could I do about this lone wolf?

The good news was, at least today he was outside and not hiding indoors.

Maybe his anti-social tendencies were easing just a bit. And maybe Zeus and I had a little to do with that. I liked that idea.

"So, hot one today, huh?" When all else failed, the weather was always good for a bit of small talk.

He leveled a glare on me. "Is that why you're here bothering me? To talk about the heat?"

Bothering him? That was harsh.

I wasn't a quitter—or maybe I was just too stubborn or stupid to take a hint. Either way, I wasn't backing down. "Actually, I wanted to see if you'd like to come on Zeus's walk. We were going to head toward the river. It's so pretty—"

"No."

That wasn't the answer I'd been expecting. I frowned. "No?"

He nodded. "Correct. No."

I shook my head, baffled. "Why not?"

His frown told me it was none of my business even before he opened his mouth. "Seriously, why the fuck are you over here all the time?"

I drew back at that.

His grumpy demeanor, I could handle. But this—this felt different. Angry. Purposefully hurtful.

I knew I could be a lot to handle sometimes. Overly sunshiny even on the darkest days. But asking if he wanted to take a walk shouldn't warrant this reaction.

Once I'd recovered from the shock of his verbal attack, I was still speechless. Meanwhile, he waited for an answer to what I guessed wasn't a rhetorical question. That being, why was I here?

I didn't have an answer for him.

Oh, I had many reasons for coming here, but not one I wanted to admit to him.

Ninth grade me had had a huge crush on Michael Timmerman, the football star and resident bad boy who drove the Camaro with the muffler so loud we could hear him from blocks away. I'd sneak peeks at him in the hallway from behind the door of my locker, fantasizing about his coming up to talk to me.

I'd fantasized about more than that too, imagining my own version of the Cinderella story where the bad boy would fall for a nerd like me, ask me on a date, and be my first kiss.

Be my first for something else too. Because if he'd asked me back then, I'd have given it to him. My virginity and anything else he wanted.

I'd have done anything for him—until he broke my heart. First, by not knowing I existed. Second by graduating and leaving town forever. Except that forever turned out to last just over twenty years and now he was back.

It was obvious why seeing him again now made the sex-deprived thirty-eight-year-old me stand up and take notice. The attraction was still alive and well inside me.

So much so I'd actually broken out the personal pleasure device my friends at the shelter had gotten me as a gag gift for my thirty-fifth birthday. Good thing there was no expiration date on those sorts of things. Even three years later, with a set of fresh batteries, it had worked just fine.

Oh boy howdy had it worked fine.

The overwhelming reality was, this was all information I needed to keep to myself. In the vault. Until death. But my libido wasn't the only reason I was here.

There was something else that kept me coming back. I really and truly believed Zeus and Michael needed each other. They were both wounded warriors. They could help each other heal.

Somehow, I didn't think Michael would like that excuse either. Which left me with a whole lotta nothing.

All I knew was I needed to say something, or risk him tossing me to the curb—literally.

"I like spending time with you," I blurted, as the deepening of his scowl flustered me.

Uh oh. Wrong answer. Anger darkened his blue eyes as he glared at me. "I don't need your fucking pity."

I drew my brows low. "It's not pity—"

"Then what is it? I never talked to you even once in my life but now, when I'm back and with only one fucking foot, you're all over me. I'm not one of your stray dogs from the shelter you have to rescue. So leave me alone." His tone was harsh. His features contorted with emotion.

My hurt was quickly replaced by anger at his

complete lack of understanding and gratitude for what I was trying to do for him.

Couldn't he see I only wanted to help?

I planted both hands on my hips as Zeus sat, pressed against my leg and let out a soft whine. "I'm not here because you only have one foot."

"No?" He scoffed. "Bull shit."

"I told you the truth. I like spending time with you."

"Yeah, sure. Because women are just lining up to go out with me since I got home."

I let out a huff. "Well, maybe if you weren't so mean and anti-social, they would be. You ever think of that? Huh? You know, it doesn't matter how hot you are if you scare everyone away."

To my surprise he quirked up one brow. "You saying you think I'm hot, little miss bleeding heart?"

Uh oh. I had said that, hadn't I?

"Um, no—well, yes, but—that's not the point," I stuttered.

He folded his arms, his stare firmly planted on me as he waited me out.

I couldn't stand the silence. I drew in a breath. "Okay, fine. Yes. I had a huge crush on you in ninth grade and it seems it hasn't completely gone away. Are you happy now?"

"Not yet, but I'm getting there." The deepening timbre of his voice cut straight through me, settling somewhere deep inside my core, filling what was empty and hollow with a feeling of warmth.

The old metal chair in which he sat scraped against the peeling porch floor as he stood.

One step, then another, put him so his body almost touched mine. He seemed even taller this close.

Then he bent, his head near mine as he grasped my chin between his thumb and forefinger.

I gasped. From his closeness. From his touch. From the one-hundred-and-eighty-degree turn this conversation had taken.

"Do I scare you?" he asked, looking as if he enjoyed the thought.

"Would it make you happy if you did?"

He laughed as he braced his hands on the railing behind me, bracketing me in, trapping me between the old wood and his hard body.

The position put him closer to me. His head lower, his mouth just an inch away for a second before he sucked in a breath and then crushed his lips against mine.

Rough. Demanding. He fisted my hair and thrust his tongue against mine. His leg was between my thighs, pressing in just the right spot to make me let out a small sound of pleasure and seek more friction.

Breathing heavily, he broke the kiss and spat, "Fuck."

I was reeling and breathless but my brain managed to register that something was wrong.

What had happened? Did he regret kissing me already?

I pulled back and glanced up. "What?"

"The old lady next door is hiding behind the curtain watching us." He tipped his head toward the neighboring house.

"Binoculars Brimley," I grit out between clenched teeth.

I scowled and, regretfully, took another step back from Michael, pissed I was being cock blocked by the self-appointed neighborhood watch.

I glanced up—way up—at him. Damn, he was tall. And handsome. And solid, his chest muscles like rocks. I liked it.

Focus. I needed to move this somewhere private. My body wasn't nearly satisfied. One kiss had only made the craving worse.

"Where's your father?" I asked.

"At the stock auction. Why?" His lips twitched with a smile. "You saying you want to come inside, little girl?"

He made me feel like a girl again. Like that fifteen-year old with a crush on him.

That crush was alive and well and unlike then, now Michael actually knew my name. And he wanted me, judging by the bulge in his pants big enough that even from next door Mary must be getting an eyeful.

I swallowed, steeled my nerve and said, "Yes, I do."

His nostrils flared as he drew in a deep breath. His gaze cut to Zeus. "He be okay if we leave him alone in the living room?"

"Yes." The word sounded breathless.

I was having trouble filling my lungs with enough air as it became apparent to me that Zeus would be alone in the living room because I'd be alone with Michael in his bedroom.

In his bed.

I swallowed hard. My belly, and parts lower, twisted with desire, as my heart pounded.

"Good." Michael looked as anxious as I was to get inside.

He turned the knob and flung the front door wide, stepping back so Zeus and I could go in first.

Mary Brimley was going to have a boatload of gossip now. And I was too damn needy to care.

5

It was like stepping back in time. The bedroom had shelves lined with trophies and ribbons. Pictures and awards. Unchanged since his graduation.

But things had changed. Michael had changed.

He stood in front of me and reached for the button on his cargo pants, but then paused. He lifted his gaze to mine.

I saw his bare chest rise and fall with the breath he drew in and blew out.

Finally, he said, "I haven't done this since . . ." He tipped his head toward the ground. "You know."

I was at a loss for the right thing to say.

There had to be a book or website or something. I needed some sort of guidance. If I said or did the wrong thing, this would be over before it began. I felt that truth to my bones.

Maybe the best thing to do was not talk at all. My mouth had gotten me in trouble before. Best not to risk it. Not now when I was so close to getting what I wanted. What I craved.

I got up from where I'd sat on the bed and walked slowly toward Michael.

With the first step, I reached for the bottom of my T-shirt that read *Mudville Shelter—We're into S&N (Spaying & Neutering)*.

I pulled it up and over my head, before letting it drop onto the floor.

The next step, I reached for the button, then the zipper of my khaki shorts, pushing them down my legs and leaving them on the floor as I stepped out of them.

I'd chosen my prettiest white lace undies and bra when I'd gotten dressed this morning. Not that I'd expected this to happen tonight. Hoped, definitely. Orchestrated, perhaps. Assumed, never. But I was glad I had them on now.

I tried not to be self-conscious as his gaze dropped to take in all of me.

My boobs could be bigger. My stomach could be flatter. My thighs could definitely be thinner and firmer.

But Michael's head-to-toe perusal didn't make me feel insecure. Quite the opposite. He made me feel beautiful. Sexy. Desired.

And my little striptease had gotten me the desired outcome. He reached for his button again, without hesitation this time and moved toward the end of the bed.

He pushed his pants down to his thighs before he sat on the edge of the mattress and pulled them the rest of the way off.

I didn't completely avoid looking at the metal that attached just below his knee, but I didn't stare either. I didn't want it to be a big deal, even though, let's be real, it had altered his life forever.

He sat and waited and watched me. I liked the idea of his watching me as I walked—strutted really—to where he sat.

I dropped to my knees and pushed his knees wider.

He planted his legs farther apart. I didn't have to work too hard to ignore the metal prosthetic. I was too distracted by Michael, half naked, aroused and ready.

I leaned in closer, my fingers hooked inside the waistband of his black boxer briefs.

He was visibly breathing heavier as I eased his underwear down. Reaching inside, I freed the hard length already straining to get out.

Michael mumbled a curse as, my eyes locked on his, I leaned down and ran my tongue over his tip.

His eyes slammed closed and his mouth fell open as I engulfed the full length of him. He palmed the back of my head and pressed deeper, groaning as he bottomed out in my throat.

"I'm not gonna last," he gasped.

I hadn't expected him to. More than that, I felt like I'd die if this man didn't touch me soon. I was definitely going to have to buy more batteries.

Cupping his balls, I quickened the pace, struggling to breathe and accommodate the length of him in my mouth at the same time.

The fingers of both hands gripped my hair as he thrust forward once, twice, three times, before the hot spurts hit the back of my throat.

We were both panting when I eased off him and leaned back on my knees.

He dropped his hold on my hair but he wasn't done yet.

Standing, he pulled me to my feet, turning me so my back was to the bed. He lifted and tossed me onto the mattress. My underwear disappeared as he yanked them down and tossed them to the floor.

Shoving my legs wide, he leaned between them and then the wait was over. The agony of unfulfilled desire was replaced by the feel of his mouth on me.

He latched onto my core while sliding two fingers inside, sending me writhing, grasping for the bedsheets, needing something, anything, to anchor me as the pleasure put me into a tailspin.

I cried out when he pressed those fingers up and sucked hard on my clit.

As my muscles clenched, I bucked beneath him.

When the spasms started, I couldn't control myself. I came so hard and loud it would be a miracle if Mary Brimley and her Miracle Ear listening device didn't hear me as clear as day.

When the orgasm finally subsided, Michael flopped onto his back next to me on the mattress where I lay boneless.

"Wow," I breathed.

He let out a breath tinged with a laugh. "Yeah."

I turned my head on the mattress. "Just so you know, if this is the result, I'm going to be here bothering you again tomorrow. And the next day. Okay?"

He rolled his head to the side to meet my gaze. "Okay."

Oh, yeah. Victory was mine. And all the orgasms—they were mine too.

The sound of a door closing had my eyes widening.

That ominous sound was followed by, "Michael!"

Oh, shit. Naked and caught by Michael's dad. Things couldn't get much worse than that.

Zeus barked and I realized things had a way to go yet before we hit rock bottom.

"Whose fucking dog is in the living room?" Mr. Timmerman bellowed before flinging open the bedroom door.

I shouldn't have been surprised at that. Cranky old

man Timmerman had never struck me as a man who would respect a closed door, particularly not in his own house.

Jesus. The situation began to fully hit me. I was half naked in old man Timmerman's house.

But I'd already foreseen this could happen, the moment I heard that door slam. And luckily, I'd rolled off the side of the bed, scooped up my clothes and was currently trying to wiggle my shorts back on while hiding behind the mattress.

Michael, thank God, had tucked himself back inside his underwear so at least his dick wasn't hanging out.

He was, however, in his room, mostly undressed, with a female. A fact that Mr. Timmerman—red-faced from embarrassment or anger, I wasn't sure—had noticed.

Cool as a cucumber, Michael bent and scooped his pants and shirt off the floor. Holding them in one fist, he met his father's glare without flinching. "The dog is Stephanie's."

That had the old man zeroing in on me as I squatted on the floor. I was dressed, finally, and apparently I wasn't hiding very well, so I stood.

Besides, I needed to clarify the situation. The next portion of my plan depended on it. "Actually, he's from the shelter. We're looking for his forever home."

Mr. Timmerman scowled as deeply as Michael had

the first time I'd said *forever home* to him. I didn't see anything wrong with the phrase. Hell, everyone used it. Everyone loved it. Everyone except for the Timmerman men, apparently.

I couldn't be concerned about that now. I had a few other things to worry about. One being I really wished Michael would put his pants on.

Finally, he sat on the edge of the bed again and began the process.

I would have thought his father would have the decency to leave. Give his adult son some privacy. He didn't.

He stood in the doorway, watching as Michael pulled his pants first up one leg, then over the prosthetic.

Michael ignored the man standing there. He stood and slipped on his T-shirt before turning to me. "Come on."

I was more than happy to go. I scurried to his side —and almost fainted when he took my hand in his.

"I'm gonna walk Stephanie home," he said, then steered me past his father, who stood speechless in the doorway.

"Bye," I said, as Michael tugged me along.

Zeus looked as ready to leave as I was. He jumped to his feet, tail wagging as he trotted to the door.

"I hear you, boy," I whispered as I hooked his leash on his collar.

Michael opened the door and waited for me and

Zeus to walk past before calling inside, "Be back later. Don't wait for me for dinner."

Did that mean he and I would be eating dinner together? I wondered as we walked to Main Street. Distracted by the question, I forgot to check if Mary Brimley was watching out her window.

I was so engrossed in the thought that I must have been staring. Michael glanced sideways at me and said, "What?"

"What what?" I asked, startled by the question.

"You're looking at me funny. Like you want to ask me something."

Only about a dozen things. I decided to stick to the one. "You're not going to eat dinner with your dad. So, uh, what are you going to be doing?"

One brow cocked up. "Don't you worry. I'll be eating something." He delivered that proclamation with a devilish smirk.

The only response I had as my cheeks heated was, "Oh."

I also might have picked up the pace a bit, but he reached out and grabbed my arm. I stopped immediately. Had I gone too fast for him?

"Wait here." With that, he sprinted across the road and disappeared into the gas station.

Apparently walking fast wasn't an issue if he could run like that.

When he returned with a small bag, held it up and

announced, "Condoms," I knew the reason for the burst of speed.

Excitement tempered my nerves and defeated any remnants of embarrassment.

This was happening. Twenty years after I thought it would, but it was happening, nonetheless.

6

"You're gonna have to tell me where you live," he said as we continued to stand on the sidewalk, not moving.

"Oh. Oh, yeah. Of course. Sorry. It's just this way." I was babbling. And he was smiling.

"You're nervous," he said.

"No," I lied.

Again Michael proved himself a master interrogator and waited me out.

Finally, I admitted, "A little."

"Don't worry that it's been a while. It's just like riding a bike."

I drew my brows low. "I never told you it had been a while."

It had, but I hadn't told him.

He laughed. "You didn't have to tell me. No woman

comes that hard or that fast if she's getting laid regularly."

"Oh, really. Well maybe it's just—just . . ." Shit. I'd argued myself into a corner.

"Just that I'm that good?" He grinned.

That was exactly what I'd hoped to avoid saying.

"Okay, fine. It's been a long while," I admitted.

"And?" he prompted.

"And you're just that good." I rolled my eyes as he laughed.

The sound had me smiling. It was good to hear him joking and laughing.

"You're not so bad yourself," he said.

"Humph. Not so bad?" I shot him a sideways glare as Zeus stopped our procession to take a whizz on a mailbox. "No man comes that fast unless it's a damn good blow job."

He let out a snort. "Trust me when I tell you, to a man, every blowjob is good, even when it's bad." When I frowned, he added, "But that one was particularly good."

"Thank you." I nodded.

We walked in silence for a moment before Michael asked, "What happened? When Zeus was injured, I mean."

I hid my surprise at the question and tried to remember what I knew. "It was an explosion."

"IED?" he asked.

"I think so."

He nodded. "Me too."

I staunchly schooled my expression. He was not only initiating conversation, he was talking about himself. About his injury. I didn't want to do anything that would make him stop.

"His handler was killed. They'd been together from when Zeus was a puppy. That, in combination with his injury and his age . . ." I shrugged. "I guess they thought it best to retire him."

Michael nodded. Quiet. Solemn almost. Until he turned and with one palm at the base of my neck, pulled me in and kissed me deep. Right there on the corner of Main and Depot Streets.

Pulling back, he asked with obvious exasperation, "How far is this fucking house?"

I laughed and tipped my chin toward the side street. "Just down this block."

"Thank God," he breathed. "Let's go."

I led the way toward the Cape Cod-style house I'd grown up in. The one I'd stayed in after my parents moved to Florida because they couldn't take upstate New York winters anymore.

They still owned it but I paid all the utilities and the taxes, which was only fair since I lived here and didn't have to pay rent or a mortgage somewhere else.

It was a pretty good deal. They visited me here. I visited them there. And now, for the first time since my taking over the house, I got to invite a man over.

Privacy was a commodity I'd never thought much about—until today, when I realized it was priceless.

I closed the front door behind us and released Zeus from his leash.

He ran to the kitchen and I heard him slurping water from his bowl.

I didn't hear much more after that since Michael had cupped my head in his big hands and was leaning low. "Where were we?"

"I believe heading for the bedroom," I said, trying and failing to sound coquettish.

He didn't seem to mind as he narrowed his eyes and groaned while he closed in on me for a deep kiss.

"Where are those condoms?" I asked, noticing the bag was no longer in his hand.

"My pocket."

I glanced down and saw the bag shoved in the leg pocket of his cargo pants. I had to think if the box fit in there, it must be pretty small. Given the heat between us, we were going to need a bigger box next time he went shopping.

Shopping.

It hit me like a bag of condoms upside the head.

He'd bought those in town. At the gas station owned by the mayor's brother. From the teenaged clerk behind the counter who volunteered at the shelter sometimes.

Holy shit. Why hadn't the horrendous enormity of the situation hit me before? I didn't know. Sex hormones had put me in a haze maybe, but it was sure clear now.

My eyes flew wide. "Holy shit, you bought those in town."

He cocked up a brow. "So?"

"So, everyone is going to know you were kissing me in front of your house and then you bought condoms. We'll be the subject of the town gossip until the new year."

He shook his head. "You worry too much. And you definitely talk too much." Michael reached up and brushed a fingertip along my lips. "I know of a much better use for that pretty little mouth of yours."

I blushed at the image that we were no doubt both remembering.

"Stephanie."

The sound of my name on his lips brought me out of my own head. "Yeah?"

"Where's the damn bedroom?" He might have donned a smartass smirk as he asked the question, but his grip on my hips, tightening as he pulled me against him until I could feel his erection, told another story.

Michael was right. I was a talker. I was a worrier. I was definitely an overthinker. But in spite of all that, I was ready to show him where the bedroom was.

"It's just this way." I took his hand and led him to the room I'd grown up in. Unlike his, it had been redecorated since then, but it seemed significant that it was inside these four walls where I'd spent so many hours thinking about—fantasizing about—the very man whose big strong hand gripped mine.

The man who'd already blown all my teenage girl imaginings out of the water with the sheer power of the reality of being with him.

The man who was about to, hopefully, surpass all of my adult fantasies too.

I heard the bedroom door close and latch. Then Michael stopped my forward progress toward the bed. He hauled me against him, my back against his front, and I knew things were about to heat up.

The warmth of his mouth on my neck as he brought his hands around to cup my breasts was further proof.

Then there was that hard length pressing into my lower back. The one I needed inside me. Like now.

After opening my shorts, he slid one hand down my belly, continuing until he hit the spot that had me gasping.

Okay, maybe I could wait a couple more minutes until he was inside me.

My legs began to quiver as he worked me hard with his hand while his mouth moved over my throat.

The heat of his breath, combined with the dirty words, spoken soft but urgent in his gruff voice against my ear, pushed me toward the precipice.

It wasn't long before I was tumbling over the edge, sagging heavily against him while crying out loudly enough Zeus scratched and whined at the bedroom door.

I was still panting when Michael spun me around and devoured my mouth with his. His tongue swept inside, claiming the territory for him and him alone.

Little did he know I already belonged to him. I think I had since that day he first opened the door and found me and Zeus on the doorstep.

"Need you," he breathed.

"Take me," I replied, hoping that heartfelt response didn't sound like a cheesy romance novel. Although when he reached down and started to take off his pants, I stopped caring about how I sounded.

I couldn't get my clothes off fast enough. This time I took everything off, crawling onto the bed completely naked. I didn't make it very far before I was tackled by an equally naked Michael.

We landed face down on the mattress. Me on the bottom. Him on top. He groaned and spread my legs with a nudge of his knee.

Thick and hard, he pushed inside. I was more than ready for this. I welcomed every stroke of his body into mine. I heard him behind me, grunting as he plunged inside me.

I wanted to see him. Watch his face. But maybe he wasn't ready for me to see him. Not if it was the first time since losing his leg.

When he reached around and worked me with his hand while he loved me, my eyes slammed shut and I wouldn't have been able to see anything even if I had been facing him rather than face-down.

I was panting and breathless when he held my hips tight and drove himself home, quivering behind me with one long, loud groan.

He was silent when he pulled out and flopped down on the mattress.

I rolled over to face him, unsure of what to say, or if I should say anything at all.

He didn't seem like a cuddler. But after what we'd just done, it felt strange to just both lay on our own side of the bed not touching.

I was torn, until Michael reached out and pulled me toward him. That question settled, I laid my head on his chest.

It wasn't in me to be completely silent so I said, "That was really nice."

He let out a short laugh. "Yeah."

I guess *really nice* was a bit of an understatement.

"Garbage?" he asked.

I glanced down and saw the used condom on his faded erection needed to be dealt with. "Bathroom or kitchen. Or, there's tissues in the nightstand drawer, if you don't want to get up."

He reached for the drawer, then froze. I lifted my head to see what the hold-up was, and saw he'd picked up my vibrator.

"*What* is *this*?" he asked, with a wide grin.

"Nothing," I answered, blushing.

"Oh, it's definitely something." He chuckled.

"Fine. It was a gag gift from a few years ago. I never even used the thing." That lie was evident since a gag gift I'd never used would probably not live, stocked with fresh batteries, in my nightstand. "Well, just once. Recently."

His eyes went dark. "When? When did you use it recently?"

I swallowed hard, suspecting he was piecing together the timeline. I tried to be vague. "I guess like a couple of days ago."

"Tell me you broke this out and used it for the first time after we met and I'm going to fuck you so hard you're not going to be able to walk tomorrow."

My cheeks burned that he'd guessed my secret, but I managed to joke, "That's not exactly a threat, you know."

"Oh, it's not a threat. It's a promise."

When he reached for the box and returned with a renewed hard-on covered with a fresh condom there was no doubt in my mind that he was going to make good on his promise.

7

The thing about really good sex is that it makes you sleepy. Just when the hottest man on earth is naked and pressed against you, Mother Nature swoops in and knocks you out for the count.

If ever there were a time I wanted to be wide awake and aware of every sensation, from the smell of his skin, to the sound of his breathing, deep and steady in sleep, it was now.

But I couldn't fight it. I fell asleep. At least I must have because the next thing I was conscious of was being startled awake by a loud booming crash.

Disoriented, I sat bolt upright in bed "What was that?"

Michael reached out for me. "Thunder. It's been rolling in for the past half hour or so."

We'd fallen to sleep with the small bedside lamp on, so I could see Michael clearly enough. "You've been awake this whole time?" I had to admit to being jealous of that.

He shook his head as another bright flash lit the sky behind the closed blinds of my bedroom. It was followed a few seconds later by another crash. This one sounding close.

"The storm woke me. You deploy enough times and you tend to pay attention to sounds like that."

Another sound reached my ears. I frowned. "What's that noise?"

Michael went still and listened. "What are you hearing?" he asked.

"I don't know. It's like a low intermittent whine." My eyes widened. "Zeus."

I fought to get free of the covers and swung my legs over the side of the mattress. I reached for my T-shirt and pulled it on without my bra. I found my underwear, also on the floor, and stepped into them while glancing up at Michael.

"The storm must be scaring him. He might not know it's thunder and not explosions," I guessed.

Michael had gotten out of bed too. He was pulling his jeans on over his underwear, which I thought was a little overdressed for just a trip to my living room, but I was too concerned about Zeus to comment on it.

Dressed enough, I ran barefoot for the door and flung it wide.

It took me a few seconds to locate Zeus. He was

cowering under the kitchen table. I pulled out one of the kitchen chairs so I could see him better.

"Hey, buddy. You scared?" I squatted down, half under the table myself as I reached for him.

I guess I didn't react to his warning growl in time. He snapped at my hand. I snatched it back with a yelp, narrowly avoiding the sharp white teeth.

"Oh my God. He just almost bit me." I lost my balance in my effort to get away from Zeus and fell with a thud on my butt.

Suddenly Michael was behind me, lifting me up.

"You okay?" he asked, turning me to face him. He took both my hands in his and looked down at them, searching for a wound.

"Yeah. I pulled back in time. But Michael. Oh my God. If he's a biter—"

He shook his head. "He's not a biter. It's just the storm. It spooked him."

Yes, the storm likely scared him. That was why he was hiding under the table. But it scared him enough to bite me? I wasn't so sure that was a good enough excuse.

Shaking, I looked up at Michael. "You think?"

"Don't worry. He'll be fine tomorrow." He glanced at the time on the wall clock. "It's late. My dad will be worrying where I am, especially with the storm. I'm gonna get going. Okay?"

I wanted him to stay. I wanted nothing more. But what could I say besides, "Okay."

The night that had started out on such a high note, was certainly ending on a low one. Michael was leaving. And I was going to be alone all night worrying about Zeus. His PTSD. His future.

Michael finished dressing and I walked him to the door and said goodnight, but I knew it wasn't going to be a good night for me.

And tomorrow wasn't looking too good either.

8

The next day, just as Michael had predicted, Zeus seemed back to his normal self.

It was me who had changed. I was more cautious. Nervous. I hesitated when putting on his leash. I took him for the shortest walk in history, afraid he might snap at another person or dog if I took him for our usual long excursion.

We rode to the shelter together, like always. He went into his usual cage. But the incident still followed me throughout the day.

I kept it to myself, not wanting to mention it to anyone there, afraid it would sink all hope Zeus had for adoption.

It was late afternoon and I was still unsure what to do about it, when Carson walked in the door.

As much as I liked the guy, he was the last person I wanted to see right now.

I huffed out a breath, letting my chin drop to my chest as I steeled my reserve to deal with whatever bad tidings he brought with him.

Finally, I raised my gaze and said, "What'd I do now?"

He drew back, holding up his hands, palms facing me. "Whoa. Relax. You didn't do anything. I've got the pet food donations from the department out in the car."

My eyes closed as I shook my head at myself. I opened them again to meet his gaze. "I'm sorry. I shouldn't have jumped to conclusions."

"It's all right. But what's going on? That wasn't like you."

No, it wasn't. I was definitely not feeling myself today. Even after a night of amazing sex with my dream man, I couldn't shake this funk.

A Mudville deputy sheriff was pretty much the last person I should tell, second only to the overzealous animal control officer. But Carson was more than a deputy. He was a friend.

I glanced at his uniform. The one that looked so good on him there'd been a few times over the years when I'd had to remind myself that I had babysat for him. That I should not be noticing how taut the fabric pulled over his ass or how his biceps bulged from beneath the short sleeves of his summer uniform.

It was that uniform that made me hesitate now. "Can I talk to you as a friend and not a deputy?"

A crease formed above his sandy-colored brow. "Of course."

I drew in a breath and said, "You know Zeus, the retired military dog who did his business on the Timmerman's lawn?"

Carson's lips twitched into a smile. "Yeah. I remember."

"Well, last night the storm spooked him. He was cowering under the table. When I reached down to try to comfort him . . . he snapped at me."

Carson nodded. "It makes sense. He's been through a lot."

"I know. And he was injured in an explosion so the loud thunder being a trigger is understandable. But if he's a biter . . ." I shook my head. "Carson, I can't adopt him out. I'm supposed to disclose stuff like this to the shelter director."

"How is he with people and other animals normally?"

"I mean he definitely prefers solitude to being around people or other dogs, but he's never been aggressive. And he's always been great with me. And he's taken to Michael Timmerman, as well."

Carson broke into a wide grin. "I heard the dog isn't the only one who's taken to Michael Timmerman."

My eyes widened. "Damn Mudville gossip."

Carson managed to temper his grin until it was just a

small smile. "Don't worry about it. Somebody will do something around here worth talking about soon enough. Then you'll be old news. But as far as the dog... I work with an organization who takes in retired police dogs. They suffer from a lot of the same issues as military dogs. I'm willing to bet if this is the first time you've seen this behavior in Zeus, it was just a reaction to the storm."

"So what do I do?" I asked.

"Next time he hides under a table, leave him the hell alone. He'll come out and look for you when he's ready to be social again. And when the time comes for him to be adopted, make sure his new family knows to give him space when he asks for it, such as when he's hiding under a table."

I felt better after having talked to Carson, even if it was more than obvious it was my own fault for not leaving Zeus alone when he so obviously didn't want to be bothered. I felt so much better that I drove directly to Michael's house instead of going home first.

Zeus deserved a nice long evening walk and I craved seeing Michael again. I craved more than just that but the rest would have to wait until we were alone—not that that would stop the gossips.

Speaking of gossips—I shot a glare at Mary Brimley's house, just in case she was creeping behind the drapes watching me, before I knocked on the front door.

Michael answered. "Hey. Everything okay? I missed you this morning."

He missed me? That was possibly the second best thing I'd heard all day. The first being that Carson thought I had nothing to worry about when it came to Zeus.

I smiled at Michael. "Yeah. Everything's great. I talked to somebody who knows about dogs who are suffering from post-traumatic stress. And he says that Zeus just needs to be left alone when he's scared and hiding. That he'll come out when he's ready."

Michael nodded as Zeus moved closer to him. "Hmm. Good advice. Sometimes you just need to leave someone alone until they're ready."

As he reached down to pet Zeus, I knew what he was saying was directed right at me and the fact I kept coming around even when, in the beginning, he'd rather I didn't.

I heard what he was saying but it didn't mean I agreed with it. I cocked up one brow. "If I had left you alone, last night wouldn't have happened, now would it?"

He sent me a sly glance. "Yeah. I guess."

No guessing about it. I was right. I was right about something else too. If I hadn't pushed my way into Michael's life, he wouldn't be petting Zeus right now, both of them looking more content together than they ever had apart.

Michael glanced up from concentrating on rubbing the dog's ear to look at me. "I want him."

"Excuse me?" I asked, confused.

"I wanna adopt Zeus."

My eyes widened. "You do?"

"Yeah."

"What about your dad? Does he even want a dog?"

"I can handle my dad. Don't worry about that."

I believed him.

I'd seen firsthand yesterday in his bedroom how well Michael had handled his father, while I cowered on the floor behind the mattress. I had confidence he'd be just as effective when it came to Zeus.

I let out a short laugh, surprised, but in a really good way. I didn't think this was the right time for a victory lap, so I managed to control myself—mostly. Well, at least on the outside.

I did allow myself a small smile as I said, "I'll fill out the paperwork."

9

As I stood at the door, Zeus by my side, I had to think how much had changed in so short a time.

The first time I'd knocked on this door I'd been royally pissed over the whole poop incident. The second time I'd been hesitant, nervous facing my schoolgirl crush.

Now—was it really only a week later?—I was confident. Happy.

I glanced down at Zeus. "You ready to move into your new home, boy?"

He looked up at me with his deep chocolate brown eyes and thumped his tail against the porch, the floorboards of which had been recently scraped of flaking paint. A new gallon of fresh white exterior porch enamel sat in the corner.

A smile twitched up my lips. If I had to guess, I'd

bet that paint was waiting for Michael to apply it. The grass was also mowed and the tall weeds trimmed around the hedges and foundation.

Many changes indeed. And even though it was making me sad to say goodbye to my canine companion, it was time for one more change.

I raised my fist and knocked.

When the door swung in, it was Mr. Timmerman who filled the open space.

I swallowed my yelp of surprise and said, "Um. Hi. Michael is expecting me."

The older man tipped his head. "He told me."

"Oh. Good. Is he, uh, around?" I asked.

Yeah, not too awkward. Right.

"He's out back putting up the last couple sections of fencing." The man tipped his head toward the rear of the house.

"We'll just walk around and—"

"Hang on. I wanted to say something to you first."

Crap. So close.

"Oh. Okay." Why did I feel as if I'd been summoned to the principal's office?

And how the hell did all the males in the Timmerman family have the power to emotionally transport me back to my awkward teen years?

"I, uh, just wanted to say I appreciate what you did. What you're doing."

Since I was pretty sure—or at least hoping—he

wasn't talking about my boffing his son I said, "I'm not sure what you mean."

"He's better. He's not quite back to being like his old self again but he's definitely getting there. And that happened when you started coming around. Thanks for being Mike's friend."

Friends. Yup, Michael and I had been *friendly* every night for the last three nights in a row. Usually more than once.

Again, that was hopefully *not* what the father of the man I was doing was talking about. And once I pocketed the embarrassment of those thoughts, I had to feel good about things. To have confirmation from family—not just my own opinion—that Michael was seeming better, was everything.

"Oh, sure. Of course. We enjoy spending time with Michael." I included Zeus in that *we*.

The man's gaze dropped to the dog. "I heard the dog has had a tough time of it himself."

What's this? Did mean old man Timmerman have a heart after all?

"He has had a rough go. But he's doing good. He and Michael get along well."

The old man nodded, but I swear I saw a glimmer of emotion, possibly an unshed tear, in his eyes.

He did have a heart even though everyone assumed he'd buried it along with Michael's mother thirty years ago. Zeus had brought the old man's heart back to life, when I hadn't even given the poor guy a chance.

That, above all of the other amazing feats Zeus had accomplished in his life and during his military career, might be this dog's biggest skill. His superpower. Healing human hearts.

"We're gonna head around back and see Michael." I tipped my head to the side of the house.

Time to get out of there, before we both started crying. That would be way more than I was ready to share with my lover's father at this time.

He nodded and Zeus and I skedaddled.

I was more than relieved to find Michael working in the yard. And that he was shirtless and looking oh so fine only added to my sheer happiness from just seeing him.

"Hi," I said.

He looked up from the tool he'd been using to attach the picket fence section to the upright post sunk in the ground.

"Hey." His smile reached all the way to his eyes as his gaze moved from me to Zeus. "My best girl and my best boy are here."

I froze at what was probably just an off the cuff expression, even though it felt like more.

He moved close and leaned in for a kiss. I accepted his quick peck on the lips happily, but I still couldn't get the question out of my mind.

After setting down the tool and ruffling the fur on the back of Zeus's neck, Michael straightened and said, "Okay. What's wrong?"

"What?" I asked, surprised. "Nothing."

"Something is up."

"How do you know?" I asked, frustrated he could read me so well all the time.

"This frown for one." He tapped the space between my brows with his forefinger. "And that you're not talking a mile a minute, like usual."

I pouted and that frown, no doubt, grew deeper. "I don't talk a mile a minute."

He cocked up a brow and waited. As usual, I caved first when faced with his silence.

"Okay. Sometimes I might," I admitted.

Again, he waited, the amused expression becoming increasingly familiar."

"Okay, fine." I huffed out a sigh. "I was just wondering, if what you said means, you know, that I am. Am I? Your girl? Because, you know, I'm fine either way. However you want. We can keep things casual—"

"Stephanie."

"Yeah?"

"Shut up and kiss me." Michael smiled wide before he pulled me in close with a hand on each of my hips.

This kiss was much more than a peck. This was a binocular worthy make-out session that I was sure Mary Brimley would be enjoying if she were home. That I couldn't care all that much if she was or wasn't was testament to how all-consuming Michael's lip-lock was.

When he finally broke the kiss and leaned back so he could see my face and I his, he said, "And, yes, you're my girl. Actually, you're my woman. And I'd better be your man." His brows drew low in warning.

"You are. The only man in my life. Believe me. Well, you and Zeus."

"Good. Let's keep it that way. Okay?"

"Okay." I smiled. I was more than happy to keep it that way for a long, long time. Possibly forever.

SMALLTOWN SECRETS

KISSING BOOKS
RED HOT
HONEY BUNS
ZERO FORKS
UNDERCOVER SANTA
MISTER NAUGHTY
DOG DAYS
BAD DECISIONS

ABOUT THE AUTHOR

A top 10 *New York Times* and USA Today bestselling contemporary romance author, Cat Johnson writes hot alpha heroes (who often wear cowboy or combat boots) and the sassy heroines brave enough to love them.

Known for her creative marketing, Cat has sponsored bull riding cowboys, promoted romance using bologna and owns a collection of cowboy boots and camouflage for book signings.

She writes full time from a Queen Anne Victorian in a small village in upstate New York that looks suspiciously like Mudville, where she tends to her backyard chickens and too many cats (but no pig).

Don't miss deals, new releases or subscriber exclusives. Join the email list at catjohnson.net/news

Made in the USA
Monee, IL
26 February 2023